BEATRICE PART ONE

SECRETS EVERYWHERE

RICHARD LEE

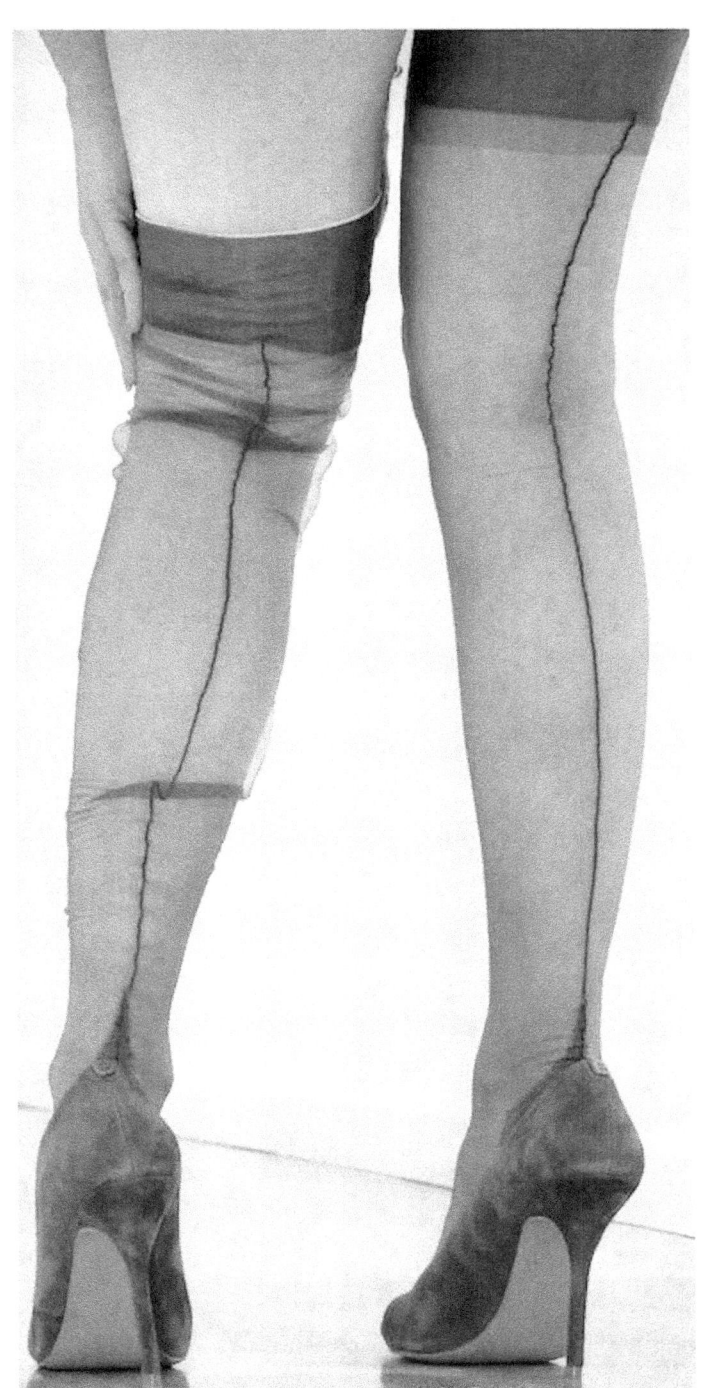

A book must be the axe for the frozen sea within us.

FRANZ KAFKA

CONTENTS

ONE

THE RECEPTION

Beatrice was impressed. It must be the wedding of all weddings. She had known that Penelope's family were wealthy, but the huge crowd at this lavish reception venue in Vaucluse, dwarfed any of the numerous weddings reception that Bea had previously attended. And being now a thirty-six year old single woman, she had attended quite a lot.

The couple were being married in a private ceremony somewhere in Double Bay.

Beatrice arrived early for two reasons. Firstly, to check the layout of the property. It would help to know what was where, and so on.

Looking around the house was exciting. Beatrice looked in all of the rooms, noticing many hidden alcoves each with beautifully upholstered sofas and arm chairs. Then she discovered a narrow back stairway leading to what must have once been the servants quarters. Doors led to tiny rooms, each housing a single bed with hardly room to move.

In the fading light, she inspected the extensive garden and noted the beautiful summerhouse and a tiny Chapel beside a pool and a fountain. It was indeed a beautiful property and she appreciated why the owner was famous for her monthly Swinger Club parties.

After checking out the reception venue, Beatrice found a comfortable settee to sit on at the end of the main hallway where she reflected on what was still to happen.

Beatrice had taught the bride in sixth form and then later, when Penny was around nineteen or twenty, they had met at volleyball where Beatrice coached a local team. Then one of Penny's cousins married one of Beatrice's cousins and thing just went from there.

Now they were close and it felt a bit like a family thing.

But what happened recently had raised tensions between her and the bride-to-be, and only after some tearful moments together, had they been reconciled.

This wedding day was important for both of them.

Penny had telephoned a week or so ago, crying and insisting that Beatrice see her immediately. Penny arrived shortly after the phone call and when she came through the door she simply stared at her friend. Then she thrust her phone towards Beatrice.

Beatrice stared at the picture on display. A good looking man wearing a big smile was looking at who was taking the picture. But what was most noticeable was that it showed fingers holding an erection which he was about to use on the rear end of a woman bent over in front of him.

But the real shock for Beatrice was recognising the woman. It was herself, standing with her hands against the Cactus Club's well known Willing Wall in the side garden.

Beatrice occasionally found herself a willing volunteer on the last Friday night of each month when she went clubbing with her girlfriends. After a couple of drinks, they might enjoy a fun interaction with one or two men, getting them excited as they acted provocatively in their short skirts and low necklines and of course, the high heels.

In the picture, Beatrice's short skirt lay on the ground along with her bra, and her knicker graced an ankle. She wore only her stockings and suspender belt and her noticeable high fashion heels.

A grinning good-looking young man stood just behind her, his cocking standing and about to be embedded in her. A woman's thumb and finger was just visible holding the base of his cock as she was taking the picture with her other hand.

It was as much as she could do to stop staring at the image. But then she looked up at Penny who's washed out face spoke of her anguish.

"I've never met Leonid, Penny; not knowingly at least. I'm guessing this is him? And Penny, I assume you know that the woman is me. If you didn't know, I'm telling you now."

Penny threw herself into Beatrice's arms and sobbed, then she tried to speak.

"I knew it was you, Bea, because of the shoes. But I wasn't sure if you knew him although I couldn't recall you'd ever met."

A silence followed broken only by Penny's sniffles.

"What are going to do, Penny? Have you shown the picture to him. And how did you get it? Will you still marry him? "

Penny sat up and wiped her eyes and nose with the back of her hand.

"It just appeared on my phone. I don't know where it came from. It's a mystery. No, I haven't shown Leo. And yes, I will still marry him, but not for love, Bea. Let me explain.

"I was at Leo's house to talk about the wedding plans but he didn't show up. I was upset and I was sitting in the sunroom with Heath, Leo's stepfather. He was angry with his stepson's non appearance, especially when Leo texted me that he'd met up with some friends in town and wouldn't make it.

"It was at that moment, the picture arrived. I could not hide my reaction and burst into tears, in fact, almost fainting and falling against Heath sitting next to me on the sofa.

"Heath took the phone from me and saw the picture. He was visibly shaken and stood up and paced the floor, yelling abuse at the wayward Leo.

"This is beyond anything I've ever seen," he shouted. "The boy is totally out of control and certainly doesn't deserve to marry a beautiful woman like you. I will strike him from my will. He will never get a penny of any inheritance from me."

"Mr Mortimer was so angry. I urged him to come and sit down so that we could talk about it and finally he fell back onto the sofa.

"I could feel his anger and his energy and for some reason I pushed myself up against him and nestled in to him to settle him a little. He put his arms around me in a fatherly fashion.

"He held me as I cried, then he lifted my face and kissed me, gently and respectfully. But then I wouldn't let him stop. His strong lips, and being in his arms were like a source of strength for my feelings of weakness. Heath gently tried to pull away but I wouldn't let him go. I wanted him so much."

Penny stopped talking and burst into a new round of crying.

"Oh Bea? What have I done? I've seduced my future father-in-law."

Beatrice took hold of the distraught young woman and pulled her close, thinking as she did so, that just when you think things couldn't get any worse, they do.

"Penny? Penny? Stop darling. This isn't the end of the world."

But Penny wouldn't have any of it.

"Yes, it is, Bea! I'm now totally in love with Heath and I know that having made love to him just once, I will want him forever. But I don't want to be a problem for him."

Beatrice took on a stronger pose.

"Stop it darling. People experience little unplanned moments and survive them. Heath is probably happy to have experienced your affection, but will now put the matter aside and concentrate on punishing his step-son in some way."

Penny sobbed and shook her head in disagreement.

"You don't understand, Bea. He made love to me for more than two hours. Can you believe it? He had me on my knees on the carpet, on my back on the sofa, up against the wall, on the piano, bent over his desk. He let me suck him, ramming his beautiful cock down my throat. I just wanted to swallow him up. Then he continued to fuck me and when he finally ejaculated, it was like a raging inferno, filling me with hot cum.

"And do you know what I thought at that moment, Bea? I thought what a pity it was that I was on the contraceptive pill. I so wanted his babies.

"Then he gathered me up in his strong arms and carried me to his bedroom and told me to rest. A little later, he came in with fruit salad and cakes and told me that he loved me and that he had a plan. Then he climbed back on me again pushing his recovered cock into me and slowly shafted my slightly sore vagina, giving me multiple orgasms. He was incredible."

Beatrice knew she was beaten. Listening to what her friend had just ecstatically described, in no way would she be able to influence Penny on this matter. She could only listen and try to be helpful.

"He has a wife, I presume," Bea asked quietly.

"They're not married. In fact Leo's mother, Svetlana, lives overseas most of the year. She spends a lot of time with wealthy Russian emigre's in London. She won't be at the wedding but she's sent a friend – I think her name is Olga, to stand in for her.

Heath refers to Svetlana's son Leo as his step-son, but legally he isn't, but having lived in the house for more than two years, Svetlana and Leo probably have certain property rights."

"So can we talk about his plan, Penny? Did it help solve the situation?"

"Well, there are options but the one he favours is that I marry Leo. That makes it possible for him to immediately include me in his will as his`` daughter-in-law.

"Heath believes that even when Leo is married he will not change his ways and this will eventually lead to a case for a divorce or maybe the annulment of the marriage.

"Either way, I would be provided for and, by living in the same house it would make it easy for Heath and I to be together."

Beatrice could see that Penny's future was planned out and her new love really did want to take care of her.

"So is there anything that I can help you with during the wedding, Penny. Can I do some little thing to help make it go more smoothly? Just ask. I'll do anything darling."

Penny smiled for the first time since she arrived.

"Well, yes there is, Bea. You don't have to agree but hear me out.

"Immediately the service finishes and we head off to the reception, Heath and I will make a quick detour to a spare bedroom in the house. We want to make love. I in no way want my new husband near me.

"I want to be with the man I love for that first time after the wedding and pretend that it was Heath that I had just married. A quickie before the speeches is what we've planned.

"If you are willing, it would help if you stood guard just in case Leo comes looking for me.

"We've arranged to meet in a room down stairs in what was once the servants quarters. They are accessible via the back garden.

"If you saw Leo searching for me and you think Heath and I are in danger of being discovered, do whatever it takes to stop him, Bea."

Beatrice stared at her friend.

"By 'anything', do I understand what you are inferring? You would want me to seduce Leo, if necessary?"

"Yes, Bea! Who better to lead him away than someone who has successfully done it before?"

It was hard to counter that argument, Beatrice agreed by silently nodding.

So the scene was set and Beatrice accepted her role as guardian of the two lovers while they enjoyed their quickie.

Beatrice didn't dare think of what might happen if she needed to confront Leo. She smiled to herself as she thought Leo probably wouldn't remember her anyway, at least not the end where her face lived.

But then she couldn't stop herself remembering how good Leo's cock felt on that Friday night. She reasoned that a repeat performance wouldn't go unappreciated. Life could be ironic.

Beatrice returned to her comfortable seat towards the end of the main hallway where it opened onto the main lounge and the adjoining dining rooms. She watched as large groups of well dressed guests arrived and spread themselves around, some pleased to find comfortable chairs, others simply standing or mingling and chatting.

Beatrice knew many of the people from the brides contingent. Most of the young ones were Penny's old school friends and Beatrice found it fascinating trying to put names to ex students, most of whom she hadn't seen since they left school three or four years earlier and now grown up.

She nodded to a few staff members. Then she spotted Elizabeth Philips, the Principal's wife along with Sandra Arnold, the Principal's secretary. They were enjoying themselves, speaking to all and sundry as people continued to file through the massive front portico.

The two seemed to get on famously and Beatrice wondered if the gossip was true, that since certain changes occurred in Elizabeth coinciding with Henry regaining his manhood capabilities.

Both his wife and his secretary were the beneficiaries of his new found vigour and complicit together in enjoying his cock's sudden return to being fully functioning.

Beatrice allowed herself a moment to reflect on all of the school gossip. Word had it that a woman had been co-opted on Mr Philips doctors advice, to help him with a very private erectile health problem.

The cure had been most successful apparently, but in the aftermath of the so-called sexual therapy, Mrs Philips had fallen totally in love with the younger woman therapist who had then gone on to show Elizabeth Philips another way of living by introducing her to Swinging.

Finally, the never ending gossip train had it that Mrs Philips was now very open to casual sexual exploits as a result of her knew lady loves swinging lessons and had developed an enthusiastic attitude to enjoying more than one cock at a time. Could that be true?

Beatrice smiled to herself and wondered what gossip there might be about herself. Given the recent events with Leo at the club and the photo, she should be prepared for the likely fall-out.

TWO

FULFILLING ONE'S RESPONSIBILITIES

Beatrice hoped that all was working out for her friends Penny and her lover. She hadn't seen them but figured they would have already managed to get to one of the little rooms downstairs as planned.

Now she had only to mingle with the other guests and watch for Leo. With a bit of luck, the not very nice young man would have gone off with friends to get drunk or play a computer game or do whatever men like him did.

Then Beatrice reminded herself that men like that frequented places like the Cactus Club, often to the advantage of lustful women like herself. Touché!

Guests had been enjoying the buffet and drinks for quite some time. Beatrice hadn't spotted any of the wedding party which seemed a bit strange.

What she did notice was the soft private school voice of the lovely Sandra who stood not far away talking to guests.

Beatrice wondered what the woman was really like and she decided to engage her in conversation at an opportune moment. And she probably should get to her before her friend, the hopefully happy Elizabeth returned from her adventures in the garden or to wherever she had lured her latest conquest.

As Beatrice moved closer to Sandra, a bell rang and a man she didn't recognise climbed up to stand where the bride and groom should have been.

"Hello everyone. My name is Percival Lemon and I'm the uncle of the bride. I'm so sorry that you have had to wait so long.

"I'm here to update you on proceedings and I hope you won't be shocked or too disappointed.

"All members of the bridal party have decamped for places unknown meaning that you will be deprived of any speeches or opportunity to farewell the bride and groom."

There was a sudden outburst of voices expressing disbelief.

"No! I cannot elaborate further. All we know is that cars suddenly appeared at the front entrance and our principal wedding participants were all driven away. I can only suspect that something dramatic happened making their appearance here impossible. Watch this space is my only advice."

There was suddenly much talking among the shocked guests.

"Now, ladies and gentlemen? I have just one more piece of information for you, this time from Ursula, the property owner.

"Ursula has considered the unusual nature of what has happened here today.

"Tonight, this venue will host its regular client who appear here at around 8 pm on the first Saturday of the month.

As the wedding reception activities have been so severely detained and it is already close to that time, Ursula, the property owner has been in consultation with the incoming group. They have generously instructed Ursula to pass on their invitation to the guests here now who would like to party-on later into the evening, that you are most welcome to stay and join them and enjoy yourselves."

Percival Lemon paused, then with a big smile, addressed the crowd. He looked down at one man who was calling out.

"No, George! It's neither the golf club nor the bowls club. It is in fact, the Sydney Swingers Club!"

Much hooting and chatter and laughter followed his pronouncement and the guests quickly forgot about the missing wedding party.

"So I won't attempt to persuade you one way or the other, but for the shy or the adventurous, it could be quite something. Thank you."

The time was already after 8 pm. Beatrice looked across to where Sandra had been standing but she wasn't there. Suddenly a hand touched her arm.

"Well, young lady. To be or not to be, or more properly, to stay or not to stay. How thinketh thou?"

The delightful Sandra was standing beside her, her eyes sparkling and sporting a definite hint of mischief.

Beatrice was suddenly excited and she fought back an urge to gasp but she was unable to prevent the blush that coloured her face.

The person she most wanted to get to know better now stood in front of her. Beatrice quickly ran her eyes over the beautiful secretary to the principal, noting her shapely body and the feet in expensive high heels.

"Oh, Sandra, I was watching you only tonight thinking how much I would like to get to know you better. Because of the new separated senior campus and tea rooms at school, we rarely see each other."

The older woman continued smiling as she took a turn looking Beatrice over and not hiding her appreciation of the smartly dressed younger woman.

"Perhaps this is a good time to do it. Are you up for staying longer and having a drink, Beatrice?"

"I certainly am, Sandra. I think they've just opened up the double doors across the passage way. It might mean that the Swingers Club bar is open. Shall we have a look?"

Beatrice was even more excited when Sandra slipped her arm in hers and found her hand and squeezed it.

Then suddenly, the forever-rushing Elizabeth appeared from nowhere and stared at them, smiling and raising an eyebrow when she saw them arm in arm.

"Hmm! Well? Now did either of you see Mr Lemon pass bye? I'd love to get his ear for just a moment."

Sandra laughed and looking at Beatrice, answered, "No! Haven't seen him, Elizabeth. Sorry!"

Elizabeth hurried off and Sandra spoke in a low voice, "It's not his ear she's after."

The two found a seat near the bar and sat down. Both were trying not to show their excitement and it occurred to Beatrice that this situation was unusual for her. Normally it was she who took someone by the hand and led them away. Having Sandra take her hand and signalling her interest was exciting. And then things got even more interesting.

They had only just sat down on the horseshoe padded seat and taken a first sip of their daiquiris when Beatrice felt Sandra's hand on her knee and a moment later felt it moving up her stockinged leg and under her skirt. She blushed again and smiled lovingly at Sandra, then she dared to put her hand on her companion's leg and soon they were both gently rubbing each others inner thighs, even opening their legs a little further to offer easier access and to better enjoy themselves.

"I could say you are leading me astray, Sandra, but I don't want you to stop. You have a heavenly touch. Please keep touching me."

Sandra's fingers moved further up Beatrice's legs and the women listened to each others deep breathing and the occasional gasp.

"I think we should finish our drinks and look for somewhere on the upstairs walkway. I was brought here once as a guest and so I know the layout quite well.

"There are a number of sofas' up there and the lights are dimmed. It's where people pass by on their way to the famous Pink Room. It's also where women meet-up before they venture off to try something else."

When the two fell onto a sofa in the wide shadowy passageway, they laid and hugged each other then excitedly moved their legs wider apart and fingered each other, embarking on a feverish kissing session. Both were already in a heightened state of anticipation so it was no surprise to either of them when each one squealed and shook, orgasming in unison.

"Oh God, Sandra! This is so beautiful. Just don't stop touching me, you gorgeous sexy secretary lady."

Sandra lifted herself and removed her knickers, asking Beatrice to do the same. Then she buried her head between Beatrice's thighs and lustfully licked and sucked her.

Beatrice quickly orgasmed.

It was while Beatrice was squealing and Sandra was sucking that two men wandered by and stopped to look at the erotic scene.

"Well, Ray. Look at those two lovelies. I suppose they are too busy to be interested in us?"

"Looks like it, Arnold. Too busy to take a poke I suppose. Never mind. Maybe we'll spot them in the Pink Room later."

Sandra heard all that was said and glanced back to see two good-looking stocky older brothers ogling her shapely backside. She quickly whispered to Beatrice that they were being checked out by two interesting males and would Beatrice be up for a quick fling with a man?

Beatrice opened her eyes and saw their admirers and quickly whispered back that she would be willing to give them a try.

Just as Arnold and Ray were about to move on, Sandra turned and smiled at them.

"Don't rush off gentlemen. Us girls fancy a bit of male attention if you are up for it?"

Arnold and Ray looked at each other and smiled.

"Damned good offer, Ray, don't you think?"

"Yes, Arnold; up against that wall would be good?"

Ray offered his hand to Sandra who graciously accepted it and stood up and Beatrice rallied herself and reached out an arm so that Arnold could pull her up from the depths of the deep sofa.

The two women were led around the back of the sofa and stood against the wall. Ray and Arnold removed their trousers and underpants, displaying their formidable cocks which lifted and swayed in anticipation.

In just moments, Beatrice and Sandra were both leant back against the wall. They had bent their legs at the knees sufficient for the two shorter men to comfortably reach and introduce their very thick cocks into two already wet and puffy vaginas.

"Oh yes! Give it to me please! Yes! Just like that, Yes!" Sandra led the ladies brigade, wanting to feed lustfully on the cocks on offer.

Beatrice screamed her excitement. 'Yes! Oh, yes! That's it!"

The two women turned their heads and smiled at each other.

Then Sandra managed to speak. "Is this what you do on Club nights, darling?"

A weak wobbly voice came back. "Yes, but its never as good as this. These men know what they are doing." Then she screamed and orgasmed just as Sandra arched her back and erupted in her excitement.

The two couples continued to enjoy their up-against-the-wall gyrations. Then Arnold looked across at his friend.

"Want to try this one, Ray. She's bloody beautiful? Lets swap. Yours looks good too."

Suddenly the two woman were cockless, but not for long.

The two men swapped Sandra and Beatrice, missing hardly a beat, and the two woman moved their bodies every which way again in their excitement.

"Oh, Sandra? These men are wonderful. They can fuck me for the rest of the night if they want. It couldn't get any better than this."

Arnold heard Beatrice's comment.

"Well, lovely ladies. We would love you to join us in the Pink Room, shortly. I for one would be happy to make love to both of you regularly throughout the evening. What do you think, Ray?"

"Yep! These ladies are beautiful. I could go all night with these two. And I wouldn't be surprised if our lovely pussy-hungry wives wanted to pinch them from us. Yes, time in the Pink Room would be great."

By the way, we should get each others names.

Everybody laughed and said their name and all promised to find each other later in The Pink Room.

Sandra and Beatrice said goodbye to Arnold and Ray, saying that they would meet up in the Pink Room shortly after they had made a quick visit to the ladies room to "check their makeup".

"We'll wait near the entrance," replied Arnold. "We are meeting up with our wives, Megan and Susannah later; most likely in the rest area. We know they would love to meet you both.

Sandra and Beatrice had a moment to chat as they used the ladies room.

"Those two are fantastic. I bet their wives are too. Can't wait to meet them," commented Beatrice.

Sandra laughed, warning Beatrice not to get too carried away with any new ladies until she had finished with her.

"Which reminds me, darling? I'd love you to come and stay at my house tonight. I'm getting in early with the invitation before you are tempted to run off with some other hot ladies."

Beatrice turned and looked at her friend, then she put her arms around her and pulled her close and kissed her and whispered, "I'd love to spend the night at your place, Sandra."

Sandra and Beatrice headed to the Pink Room and as they approached, they read the sign on the door.

Important! No pics or phone calls allowed. Text messages only. Offenders evicted. Lockers here: Stilettos, tights, glasses, shoes and other excess clothing.

They quickly opened and shared a locker, at the last moment, remembering to remove their knickers and leave then with their shoes. Then they moved towards the door in stockinged feet.

Arnold and Ray were waiting in their colourful socks and took the two by the hand and led them into the crowded room, finding a spot on the carpet that was barely big enough for the two couples.

All around, people were in a state of rapture. Bodies heaved and moaned. Men and women were making out like there was no tomorrow. It could only be described as hectic.

Some women were lifting themselves up and down on mens cocks while quite a few others humped between the legs of a willing females while at the same time, offering their rear ends to whoever chanced upon them. Mostly, though, men were feasting in doggy-style.

"Now you lovely men! You've seduced us once already. So before we meet your wives and fall in love and run off with them, we would love you to seduce us again. On our knees first, perhaps?"

Sandra and Beatrice smiled lovingly at Arnold and Ray. Then they knelt down on the cherry-pink carpet amidst the bodies of people too busy to notice them.

Arnold and Ray knelt down behind the two women and lifted their skirts and stared at two beautiful backsides.

"We must have done something right to deserve this, Ray."

Having each other for a second time was especially enjoyable for the women. Simply by knowing the men made them feel more relaxed and more in control of their situation.

Sandra looked across at Beatrice and they shared happy smiles of satisfaction as the two thick solid cocks massaged their special spots for a second time, causing little tremors to each vagina along with the promise of something more.

Sandra reached a hand across and caressed a breast and Beatrice joyfully returned the favour. But then both women heard a familiar sound.

The haughty private school voice of the horsey Elizabeth Philips floated around the immediate vicinity of the two women and they looked across to their left to view their friend moving happily at a steady canter.

Elizabeth was riding Percy Lemon's cock. But not only was her pussy impaled on Mr Lemon's member, a new cock had arrived and presented itself between her buttocks. A rear-end entry was about to be enacted.

"Its well lubed so you shouldn't have any trouble," called the insatiable Elizabeth. "Try to synchronise your movement, would you please? I do enjoy synchronised double-dipping. Not too fast, thank you. Slower is much more enjoyable."

Sandra and Beatrice watched as the newly arrived man presented and inserted his impressive member between Elizabeth's buttock cheeks.

"Oh yes, that is very good. Superbly done, you! Now give it to me. Take your time. I'm happy to be shafted like this for the rest of the day. What is your name, by the way?"

Sandra and Beatrice reached across to each other and smiled and held hands, closing and opening their eyes blissfully as the super cocks of their two men pleasured them for the second time that day.

First Beatrice and then Sandra, pushed backwards and upwards and orgasmed, screaming out their excitement as the two men riding them exchanged satisfied smiles.

And when the two women came, hands reached out from women laying close bye, touching each of them in a show of mutual and complicit affection and muttering, "Yes darling."

Sandra and then Beatrice responded, reaching out to touch their neighbours, fully appreciating other women's thighs and breasts and their endearing words of support.

THREE

ELIZABETH GETS A PRESENT

Beatrice stood quietly, watching for any sign of Leonid or of Penny. Then she became aware that she was not alone. She looked up at four handsome smiling young men, all of whom were staring at her appreciatively, each with an expectant questioning look.

Beatrice stood up, taller than most women but still not as tall as a couple of the men. She laughingly stood and looked closely at each in turn, putting aside her fear that she was about to be confronted by an admirer from her recent exploits at the Cactus Club.

"Hello! Beatrice Duncan isn't it? You might not remember me? I'm Rory and I used to sometimes watch you when you were coaching my sisters?"

"Yes, of course I do. Rory Slater? So good to see you. How are Trinity and Claire?

The three young friends of Rory smiled and laughed while eyeing up the super attractive woman who they didn't believe that Rory really knew but now realised that he had been telling the truth.

"They are well and both looking forward to getting back to playing volleyball after the holidays."

Rory then turned and introduced his friends.

"This is James, Graham and Felix. We play basketball together."

The good looking young men all smiled and nodded and Beatrice couldn't help but notice that they all gave off an air of expectancy, but for what she was not sure, although it wasn't hard to guess.

Their excitement at meeting who they thought was the most attractive woman in the room was obvious and their comments alluded to Beatrice's attractiveness. Each took turns in trying to outdo the superlatives of the boy who spoke before them, and Beatrice couldn't help but colour-up, trying to hide the pleasure she was experiencing from the adulation of such attractive young men.

"Now stop that, boys. Flattery will get you into trouble if you're not careful. Now I'd love to get to know you all but I've got to meet someone in a few minutes."

The boys all groaned.

In response to much prodding from his three friends, a red faced Rory blurted out, "But Miss Duncan? We were about to ask if we could show you the garden and even the summer house. It would be such fun. Surely our offer must be better than the one you've got already?"

Looking at the handsome young men, Beatrice could see that heading off with them out into the late afternoon to wander in the garden could be wonderful, even exciting, but she had responsibilities. She fumbled in her bag for a moment then proffered a tiny notebook and a pencil.

"I'd love to catch up with you, believe me. Write down your names and phone numbers and I promise I'll be in touch. I would love us to get together."

As the four young men enthusiastically wrote down their details and handed them over, Beatrice looked down the hallway. Then she turned and spoke in almost a secretive whisper.

"Now, Rory. I might be able to help you and your friends with your idea of walking a lady out to the summerhouse."

A sudden silence descended over the young men and they leant in closer to hear, while breathing in the heady perfume of Miss Duncan's cosmetics.

"Now try not to make it look too obvious but you could be well rewarded by approaching the tall lady down there near the potted plant, talking to her friend.

"I have it on good authority that she would just love to join a group of good-looking young men and be taken to inspect the summerhouse. She might even be looking for something more. I know she looks considerably older, but believe me, she does have a reputation with younger men.

"Please don't tell her I sent you. Her name is Elizabeth and her friend is Sandra. It might not work, but it could. Best of luck. Oh yes, and for God's sake, just don't utter the word Cougar.

"Now I'd better get going. I'll call each of you! I'll be looking forward to seeing you all in the future. Bye!"

As the young men turned to leave, Beatrice slipped away, not wanting to be observed talking with the four likely bringers of good cheer to Elizabeth.

Beatrice moved further down the hallway and looked around her, trying to see if Leo was about.

Then she retraced her steps, just in time to peep around a doorway and witness Elizabeth slip her arms into the arms of two of the gang of four and be led away, smiling profusely at her good fortune.

From a distance, Beatrice could see how hot the lads looked and she smiled to herself and thought about her plan to contact them individually. "Just one or maybe two at a time would suit me fine," she mused.

Offering them the Principal's wife for starters was a good move in preparation for her own later enjoyment; and it would be interesting finding out just what the recently liberated Elizabeth had taught them.

FOUR

SUMMERHOUSE HEAVEN

Elizabeth and Henry were attending the wedding of one of the schools older students, Penelope and her new husband, Leonid.

Elizabeth had arrived with her husband and her husband's secretary, Sandra, recently a recipient of the newly rejuvenated Henry's mojo.

At the last minute, late on the previous Friday afternoon, the smiling secretary inquired after Henry's newly found zest for life following his therapy.

She timed the question to coincide with her bending over in her short tight fitting skirt to change the date page of her desk calendar. Her bosses response could not have answered the question better.

Henry mumbled that things were just fine and that maybe she would like him to show her just how successful his therapy had been.

As Sandra was about to turn and invite him to tell her, Henry simply lifted her skirt and pulled aside the crotch of her panties and suddenly Sandra yelled and moments later found herself moaning with satisfaction as Henry energetically shafted her forever moist vagina.

Then they both came; all in the twinkle of an eye.

Sandra turned and smiled. Thank you, Mr Nichols. I hope you

enjoyed that as much as I did. Then she turned, collected her coat and handbag from her chair, and left.

Sandra decided that quickies like this were actually very satisfying and well worth encouraging.

And thinking ahead, after having had a recent and intimate conversation about their school days in England, Sandra was also in line to become Henry's wife's lover, too.

The reception was being held at a large mansion in Vaucluse and Elizabeth and Sandra were enjoying meeting a number of the guests who were known to them through the school.

When Elizabeth cheerily accepted the offer made by four very attractive young men to accompany them on an expedition to discover the summerhouse, she didn't think it happened for any other reason than the four found her really attractive.

Elizabeth quickly learned each of the young mens names and she also noted each ones more obvious attributes and their sense of themselves. If there was uncertainty about anything, she thought, it was simply each young man's level of sexual maturity.

Elizabeth was her usual hungry self in search of a sexual encounter. Were these lads all too nice and still too innocent to act suggestively towards her? She needed a plan.

Her sexual liberator, mentor and now lover – Angie – wasn't here to advise as she was when first she took the newly liberated Elizabeth to the exclusive dogging venue at the Sydney Golf course, advising her what to do when cocks first appeared, stiff and waving at the car window; or then, when she first groomed her on the art of swinging and the use of lubricants should an anal suitor request that she roll over and offer him access to her derrière.

Elizabeth figured that in this situation, Angie would have urged her to take a direct approach, especially given the limited time she could be away from the wedding festivities without her absence being noticed.

Four quickies would be ideal if she could manage the young men to do the deed. The direct approach is the path she chose.

The sun was getting lower in the sky as the group of five entered the summerhouse.

"Well, boys, here we are. It's lovely here isn't it? It's the sort of place you might bring a new lover. I know its where I would love to be brought for a bit of a cuddle and hanky-panky. Look at the sofa and all the cushions. There couldn't be a better spot for lovers to stretch out."

Elizabeth plonked herself down in the middle of the sofa and looked up with her finest come-hither smile. The men were all looking at her, not quite believing what they were hearing and unsure what to do. This was outside of the experiences that any of them had encountered in life. Elizabeth was a fantasy lady and she couldn't possibly be real?

Elizabeth smiled up at each of them and then she slowly unbuttoned her top and pulled it open, happily aware that she was being stared at. Then she pulled down her bra so that her large shapely breasts hung over like fruit waiting to be harvested.

Elizabeth's large stiff nipples stood out and captured the ever widening eyes of her audience.

"I think you should grab this opportunity to grab me and have some fun. I'm definitely up for it if you lot are? What do you think?

"Whose going to be first to put their hands on my lonely tits and nibble my nipples. And who will be first to show me their cock? I do love cocks. A girl can't have enough cocks. The more cocks the better. In fact, why don't you all get out your cocks while I take off my skirt and get myself ready for you all?"

If there had been questions or doubts from either James, Graham, Felix or Rory it was now far too late to think about them.

The vision of the voluptuous Elizabeth prostrating herself on the sofa, offering lots of bare flesh and wearing only her knickers, suspender belt and stockings and high heels, was an opportunity not to be wasted by four hesitant young men who had only ever seen the likes of this on internet porn sites.

Four cocks appeared, already stiff and rising, and trousers were discarded and Elizabeth was soon calling them all to, "Come and have some fun, boys. I promise I won't bite. Well, maybe I will just a little bit."

"Oh, God! You are all magnificent. Here James, let me suck you first. And Felix and Rory? Let me hold your cocks, and Graham, pull off my knickers, you darling man and push my legs apart and slip your cock right up inside my wet pussy. I want us all to go to heaven together."

The four young men fell totally under Elizabeth's spell and they never regretted it. Never had they experienced what this beautiful older woman was doing with them. The more she handled their private parts, the more they wanted to possess her. And they did. Or was it really Elizabeth possessing them?

Elizabeth led the action in any way she wanted it. Her mouth was rarely without a cock in it even as she rolled over on the sofa or knelt on the carpet and pushed up her backside, calling out, "Who wants to try it this way? This is called the doggy position. I love being fucked this way."

Then she stood up against the wall, her knees bent slightly while pushing her pelvis forward and plaintively urging everyone to "Fuck me some more please. I promise you will love it."

As time moved on, Elizabeth reasoned that her cock play should draw to a close by letting each boy cum, either in her mouth or in her vagina and that would be easy to arrange.

All four musketeers called out as they came, each enjoying the ultimate final sharing moments of Elizabeth's cock heaven.

Bodies littered the floor or drooped over the sofa arm. Elizabeth licked the remains of sticky stuff from her lips and in a gentle low voice, gave her last command.

"If you boys enjoyed yourselves and would be happy to pleasure me again with your beautiful cocks, please write your names and phone numbers down for me and I'll get in touch. You have all been so wonderful. It would be good to do it all again, don't you think?"

A chorus of voices called back confirming that four newly initiated young studs would enthusiastically attend to Elizabeth's every future desire.

"Thank you. Now we'd best get back. I need to use the little bathroom here to put myself together again. You four head back. Who knows, there could be ladies like me looking out for lads like you this very minute, so don't delay."

The four men all burst out laughing then one voice called out.

"I think you've given us enough to keep us going for quite awhile, Elizabeth. What we need now is food. Three cheers for the sexiest lady in the world."

Elizabeth laughed and called out a "thank you, boys" as the happy lads cheered and as she headed to the bathroom and stared at her radiant, if dishevelled self in the mirror and smiled.

"Oh, that every day could be like this one."

FIVE
GUEST WITH BENEFITS

Amongst the wedding guests who laughingly decided to take advantage of the Swingers Club offer for them to share their evening with the club, three couples excitedly waited to see what went on.

Dressed in their immaculate wedding attendee clothes, three husband and wife couples wandered slowly around the large room where the wedding party had meant to be hosted. That was before the announcement that all of the members of the wedding had absconded to no one knew where.

All three women had been friends of the bride's late mother who unfortunately died at an early age.

In an effort to ensure that the wedding was a big one, everyone who was ever associated with the brides family were sent invitations.

Two husbands in the party were already tipsy as was one of the wives.

Glenyce's husband didn't drink but he was happy for his wife to imbibe at functions like this.

The truth was that Glenyce drove Gerald crazy most of the time and they were not happy together.

She was quick to criticise others and she constantly harped on about him not being as attentive as other women's husbands.

When she had had a few drinks, Glenyce tended to interact more with other people. And despite her Welsh name meaning pure and holy, she could be quite amorous towards other males.

Gerald was very tolerant, and never interfered with whatever Glenyce was up to. In fact he enjoyed having a little time to himself when he could chat happily to others, especially other more friendly women.

It wasn't that Gerald was a womaniser, far from it, he was normally quite shy. It was just the enjoyment of being with the men's wives, Andrea and Margo, who were polite and charming and uncritical.

When word came of the Swingers Club offering to share the evening with the wedding guests, Gerald and his friends were more than happy to linger longer.

The party of six moved slowly around the venue and it wasn't long before they had become separated into two groups. Those who were drinking and those who were not.

Andrea and Margo seemed especially excited to be in the middle of an event they had never experienced before and they acted in a way that suggested they knew something about swinging but only a little, and that each was eager to learn more.

"This could be far more interesting than the wedding, anyway," Margo announced as she looked at a woman who had a man's hand slowly feeling her backside through her skirt while the woman cupped her hand over the front of his trousers.

The three realised that there were now more people from the Swingers Club in the reception area than there were wedding guests.

"I'm not sure if I should be here?" commented Gerald, pretending to be nervous. But then a woman approached him and smiled. She was minus her skirt and her silky stockinged legs balancing on stilettos marked her as a Swinger Club member.

"I hope I'll see you in the Pink Room later, sweetie." Then the woman put her hand where Gerald's tackle was hiding and squeezed him.

"And bring your girlfriends with you. They look like they would enjoy themselves. They look gorgeous. They look like they would enjoy a bit of me, too."

The three watched, open mouthed as the hot number moved off through the crowd touching up male and female fellow members of the club, sometimes kissing them and whispering something in their ear.

Margo and Andrea looked at each other and burst out laughing.

"Now you are really in trouble, Gerald. We will make you escort us to the Pink Room whatever happens. Our horizons have already been widened by that sexy lush; and we would both like to know her better, don't you think, Andrea?"

Andrea looked at her friend. "Do you think he'll manage two turned-on women in whatever the Pink Room is, Margo? Do you think that together, we will be able to make Gerald feel less nervous?"

"I'd say he will love it. Now that Glenyce has disappeared with our inebriated spouses, Gerald will jump at our offer to look after him in the Swingers Club."

Everyone laughed and Gerald, for just a moment, saw his companions in a different and more exciting light and joined in their laughter.

Unbenknown to Gerald or his wife, Margo and Andrea had only recently come to the decision that their husbands were not worth the effort, and, wanting to break out of their restrictive married-woman mold, they had taken the advice and practical instructions from a neighbour.

Susannah, a friend from the next street, had invited them around for afternoon tea. She had her close friend Megan with her, and the ladies were soon enjoying girl talk.

When Margo had let slip that things were not good at home and Andrea had confirmed the situation was the same situation at her house, Susannah smiled at Megan.

"Shall we tell them Megan? Are they ready, do you think?"

"Or maybe we could show them, Sue?"

Susannah then told her guests about she and Megan's recent adventures at the Swingers Club and how it had changed their lives and also their husbands lives.

Then they turned to each other and kissed, then they kissed some more.

Margo and Andrea were in awe of what their friend was telling, and now showing them.

Susannah and Megan stopped kissing and Susannah looked at her confused and blushing visitors.

"It was a shock to us to begin with. Now we get together regularly and have special girl time. And it doesn't end their. We've also learnt to enjoy other men as well. Our husbands are on board and now enjoy each of us; swapping the two of us with loving care and devotion.

"And they too, with our approval I should add, will sometime swing with other women at the Swingers Club. We are all so lucky."

There was a prolonged silence as Margo and Andrea tried to process what they had just heard and witnessed. The evidence was in front of them. It looked as though a different way of looking at life could be very rewarding.

Andrea coughed and cleared her throat.

"I think Margo and I are impressed and, for myself, your way of doing things definitely appeals to me. But I suspect you have more understanding husbands than us and I can't see how we could ever include them. Actually, I don't thing I would want to, to be honest."

Margo entered the conversation, nervously but determined to have her say.

"Like Andrea, I'm impressed and I agree with her that our husbands should probably not figure in anything we might choose to do. In fact, sad as it sounds, we do need to get away from them"

Silence prevailed as all four women considered the situation. Then Margo whispered, "How do we begin? Your help, Susannah, would be appreciated."

Susannah looked around at everyone and smiled. Then she stood up.

"Its really quite simple. Just spend a little time with us.

"Megan, can you take Margo and I'll take Andrea. Lets get these lovely gals liberated."

Susannah and Megan stood up and reached forward and each took a hand of one of the two nervous women.

First they folded their arms around each one and squeezed them, then Susannah led Andrea out of the lounge and into the nearby sunroom, first pulling the heavy curtains across and then sitting down on a little day bed.

Then, neither waiting nor with small talk, Susannah folded Andrea in her arms and brought their mouths together and seconds later, both tongues were dancing together, and Andrea found herself where she had wanted to be for so long but hadn't known how to get there.

Meanwhile, Megan took Margo by the hand and led her to a spare bedroom. She lowered the two of them onto the single bed and then lay on top of Margo and looked into her eyes.

"You are beautiful," she whispered. Then she kissed the nervous woman who eagerly responded, quickly, desperately attempting to suck Megan's tongue from her mouth.

Two frustrated unhappy wives lives changed suddenly. Both fought for more of what Megan and Susannah was giving them, unclipping their bras, lifting themselves up to be relieved of their knickers, and pulling the buttocks of their liberators down onto them as they humped the newbies all the way to heaven.

Occasionally one would hear a distant scream from the room next door, signalling a high moment. Nothing could have been better than what Andrea and Margo were experiencing. This was truly their moment of liberation.

And when they all eventually emerged and found their way back to the lounge room sofa, the excited Andrea and Margo grabbed each other and fell onto the sofa with their lips together and their hands on each other in every possible secret place.

And when the two wives stopped and looked up, they watched in wonder as Susannah and Megan leisurely enjoyed each other on the carpet in the classic 69 position. Then Andrea and Margo continued feeling each other every which way and kissing, neither wanting the day to end.

SIX

WILL IT WORK FOR ALL?

In Margo and Andrea's households, stunned husbands knew better than to ask questions when their wives told them that they and their girl friend would be away for two nights on secret womens' business.

"Enjoy your freedom, darlings. We won't be round to nag you."

The women had booked themselves into a fancy hotel where every luxury was available; room service, the heated pool, a sauna or a massage. But what was most important was their freedom to be alone together.

They laughed and cried and humped and licked and slapped and nipped their way to heaven at least a half a dozen times each day. And they slept in total harmony .

Margo and Andrea's liberation was now complete. Or was it?

The wedding reception had turned into a very different event when the incoming Swingers Club invited disappointed wedding guests to stay on into the night and join in the Swingers Club revelry.

The original group of six was now two groups of three. One lot were drunk and the others cold sober.

Glenyce and her friends inebriated husbands – Harry and Trevor – eventually found their way up the stairs to the Pink Room, but the smiling man and woman at the door, who, in a most friendly fashion, administered each a breath test, turned them away and the three stumbled further long the dimly lit passageway.

Harry retrieved his hip flask and took a swig of Bourbon and passed it to the others. As Glenyce took a swig, Harry looked at her sexy legs and her substantial breasts and ventured a comment.

"Trevor? I reckon Glenyce should give us a bit of something? I reckon she would enjoy a bit of fun. We don't need the bloody Pink Room."

The three had fallen onto one of the many three seater sofas that lined the walls and Glenyce knelt with her face down on the seat between the two men, trying to work out what was happening.

There was silence. Then the raspy alcohol flavoured voice of Glenyce confirmed that she had heard what Harry had said.

"What a good idea, Harry. Get your cocks out and I'll give you both a blow job. You'll have to buy me drinks later, though. I'm not for free."

It took a while for her companions to understand what she was offering, but then the two fumbled with their trousers and let out two small limp cocks.

Glenyce sat up and looked at what was being offered.

"Hell! A girl's got her work cut out getting these up. You had both better feel me up and play with my tits. That might get you going."

Glenyce lifted herself and shed her knickers. Then she took off her dress and shed her bra and lay back with just her stockinged legs and suspender belt and shoes on display.

"Now get into me, fellas. I'm feeling horny just looking at myself. And if you can get your cocks up I'll let you both fuck me. Would you like that?"

Two sleepy men murmured that they thought that would be really good.

But try as she may, Glenyce could not get the mens cocks to stand, and not only that, the men kept dropping off to sleep.

"You two are bloody hopeless. What's a horny girl supposed to do?"

The answer to a girls prayer was answered when two men and a woman wandered up to the three on the sofa.

The men seemed sober but were holding up a woman who seemed totally out of it.

When they peered through the darkness and observed the near naked Glenyce, they called out.

"Hey gorgeous? Would you like to swap places with our friend."

It took less than a moment for Glenyce to agree and she helped the men to make the woman comfortable on the sofa between Harry and Trevor. Then she looked at the men and smiled.

"Find us somewhere comfortable, gentlemen. I'm desperately wanting stiff cocks to fuck me right through the night. Happy with that?"

Glenyce could already feel hands rubbing her butt and her pussy and when she searched the two trouser fronts, she found hard-ons that promised her what she craved.

"This way, sweetheart. We know where there is a little room with a bed. You will be very comfortable. I'm Ron and that is Alby. What is your name?"

"Pleased to meet you both. I'm Glenyce and I love it that you both have hard-ons."

Glenyce observed that she was now totally sober and that the idea of two cocks to play with was going to make her very happy.

Tonight was going to be really good after all. And interestingly, it was the last night that Glenyce ever took a drink.

———

Gerald thought that his companions seemed a little different from the last time he'd seen them. He realised that he hadn't in fact, seen them for a number of weeks.

"You both seem particularly happy with yourselves tonight. Is it because you've got rid of your spouses?"

Gerald's attempt at off the cuff humour was noticed.

"We might not tell you why we are happy, Gerald. Maybe it's the good company?"

"No, Margo. Lets not tell him. Let's show him."

Andrea and Margo laughed in a way that made Gerald feel happy and secure. Was this what real friendship was like, he wondered?

Margo and Andrea each put an arm under Gerald's and clasped a hand.

In the ladies rooms earlier, the two had confessed that having got to this stage in their emotional liberation, it was probably time to add a missing element to their new found sexual freedom. And the two had agreed that if there was to be a man involved, then it should be Gerald.

"He deserves better."

"Yes! That bitch of a wife will never change, just like our husbands will never change."

The two were silent as they added new lipstick. Then Margo, speaking in a low voice said, "I bet she'll be trying to fuck both of our husbands right now except she'll find they are too drunk. Best of luck with that, Glenyce."

How to get Gerald to join in their love-making was now the big question. Should it be tonight or should they think of something else.

———

It was now close to 10 pm and the crowd in the reception area were predominantly Swinger Club members.

As Gerald looked around, he could see that Swinging was what everyone was doing. He watched as a woman bent over the back of a sofa with her skirt pulled up while another woman lazily pulled down her panties and felt between her legs with one hand while massaging a buttock with the other.

Gerald wondered what Margo and Andrea were thinking and looked to see if they had noticed the women.

Gerald's world was suddenly turned upside down. His friends were watching the same two women but not only that, Margo had lifted up the back of Andrea's skirt and her hand was moving around on her buttocks inside her frilly knickers. And the happily complicit Andrea had slipped a hand inside Margo's top and was busy massaging a breast.

When the two women realised that Gerald was staring at them, they smiled lovingly and Margo leant towards him and kissed him on the lips.

"Yes, Gerald! Andrea and I have made changes. We were not sure how to tell you but now you can see. And we are very happy.

"We've even left our husbands and moved into an apartment together. The only reason Harry and Trevor are here is because their names were on the wedding invitations.

Gerald tried to get his head around what he was hearing and seeing.

Andrea passed him a piece of paper with their new address.

"We want you to visit us, Gerald. Say you will! Please?"

While Gerald tried to get things clear in his head, Margo added a bit more.

"And Gerald? We have a lovely spare room with a big comfortable bed so you can even come and stay with us. We would so love that, wouldn't we, Andrea?

Gerald suddenly had an epiphany.

Andrea and Margo were not just friends. They represented intimacy in a way he had never before realised.

Hiding himself to cope with Glenyce's constant attacks on him had cut him off from his feelings. Andrea and Margo's friendship could change that; it could release him from a way of life that he had unwittingly fallen into.

Gerald looked at Margo and Andrea and smiled. A tear formed in the corner of his eye. Then he embraced each of them, whispering 'thank you'.

When he stood back, smiling a smile that they had never seen before, Gerald looked at this piece of paper.

"I will definitely visit you; very soon, in fact. Thank you both so much."

SEVEN

WHEN TO STOP?

Margo and Andrea's new life together meant that all lifestyle possibilities were available for their investigation.

Having just moved into the second half of their forties and now, having left their husbands and moved in together, the two women were seeking to expand their boundaries. And it seemed that the choices were limitless.

While so intimately exploring each others bodies and emotions, they came to the conclusion that they were both still young and they should look at their lives in a new way.

Firstly, they discussed buying new clothes.

Their liberator, Susannah, had mentioned in passing that the two had great bodies and that they shouldn't hide them.

"You need younger wardrobes, darlings.

"Think about getting new clothes. You won't regret it. Oh yes! And maybe try looking at some porn. You'll get lots of useful information there, and not just about clothes."

Margo looked at Andrea and smiled weakly.

"Looks like we are going to have a busy time, Andrea. Where on earth do we start?"

They began with social media, discovering a world of fashion on

Instagram along with lots of sites that told them that when it comes to girls being with girls, they were definitely not alone.

That was comforting, as were the many entries on positive self image for women in their age group. The word 'hashtag' was suddenly the doorway to a world they hadn't known about.

Looking at pornography was a different thing altogether. The more popular providers offered thousands of videos, mostly enlightening and unexpectedly, fun.

Over a number of evenings, cuddled up on the sofa with the laptop, Andrea and Margo gained ten years of sexual experience in just a few nights.

Margo was renowned for yelling at the television set, giving advice or demanding justice. She did the same with the internet.

"OMG! How does she do that?" and "No way! He can't be serious, surely." And that was just cruising the initial popular offerings.

On the second day, things became bosom fixated.

"He can't possibly think they are real, surely to God?"

On the third day the two discovered that a woman can also be wanted for her rear end.

"No! Get up, woman. He will never fit that huge thing in there." To which her up-till-then silent girlfriend added. "Interesting though! It might be fun, Margo?"

On the fourth day they became more porn savvy and entered search terms. The two women discovered Gay Male porn and watched in awe, things they never thought possible.

"What a body and what a waste," was most often the comment they made.

On the fifth day they found Lesbian porn and realised that the multi-faceted layers of human interactions was indeed, complex and extraordinary. They also noted that sex aids came in more shapes and sizes than they ever realised, and that certain vegetables could some-times come in handy.

On the sixth day Margo tapped on a link which found them looking at beautiful transexuals, most of whom seemed to be looking for love.

"I'd help any one of them, for sure."

On the seventh day, Andrea typed in 'bisexual women' and they were suddenly home.

Women pleasing women and sometimes a man at the same time. Margo and Andrea squeezed each others hands, resting comfortably between their legs.

Then came something that changed their life.

Andrea clicked on what looked like an interesting video and suddenly, fisting came into their lives.

The on-screen woman seemed intent and sincere in her appreciation of having her girlfriend's hand right up inside her vagina, touching her womb while she gently gave the loving provider instructions.

"In further, please darling! Now make a fist! Now turn it gently to the left. And now to the right."

And it wasn't just women with women. A man's hand could be equally welcomed.

Margo and Andrea just couldn't get enough of the super explicit fisting videos. The two women were so excited. Eventually they switched everything off and sat back and looked lovingly at one another.

"The top of our to-do list, Andrea?

"Definitely! I'll get more lube in the morning, darling."

Andrea and Margo shopped for clothes on line and also wandered around an online sex shop.

Then they dressed in their best street clothes and went to town and shopped.

They tried things on and called each other into the changing rooms to look and pass an opinion.

"I do like these short camisole slips, Margo. What do you think. Can you see me in it along with my new stocking and garter belt and high heel?"

"OMG that is so hot! But would you dare wear it, Andrea?"

"Only for you, darling. Or maybe we should join the Swingers Club? I could be quite a hit, there."

Margo and Andrea each purchased three camisole slips. Two short ones and, then at the last minute, a long one, "just so as not to draw too much attention to ourselves."

Stockings, underwear, shoes, dresses and skirts and tops filled their bags. Over three consecutive days, they spent a fortune, determined to make a difference to their wardrobes. And with the final addition of shorty pyjamas and elegant dressing gowns, and sexy bedroom slippers with fluffy fronts and little heels, they couldn't think of another thing they needed.

"The only thing we need now, darling, is someone to show off too. Which brings me to the invite that came in the mail from the Sydney Swingers Club.

"I've no idea how their algorithm works, but they knew we had both just turned forty-five, the minimum joining age for women.

"Apparently, it's only forty for men. That is to make sure that the girls have plenty of active males to pick from I suppose. A good idea, don't you think?"

Margo looked intently at her lover. "Well, Andrea. I'm up for a little bit of boy stuff if you are. It's been so long, I've almost forgotten what it might be like. My husband was never much to start with and it only got worse, the more he drank."

"Same with me, Margo. So do you think we could leave each other alone long enough to play with something neither of us have?"

Margo reached out and grabbed Andrea and smothered her with kisses, dragging her down onto the carpet and laying on top of her.

"Well! I suppose we shouldn't deny men the benefits of our super bodies and our new wardrobes. Yes, lets join up."

Margo automatically went into a humping motion and Andrea lifted her legs and bent her knees and joined in the dance of love.

"From what we saw on the night of the wedding, apart from the exciting bits, that is," panted the humping Margo, "all the Swingers – men and women – seemed nice enough. And although we've said that Gerald should be the lucky first, I don't think we should bet on him making us an offer we can't refuse. He's got too much to think about."

"Yes, you are right, gasped Andrea. Short of putting the hard word on him directly, Gerald might have to be something on the side, if and when it happens. We girls need to struggle on."

Andrea's deep breathing suddenly changed to a panting scream as she threw herself up to meet her love.

Life couldn't be any better for these two.

EIGHT

A NOT-FOR-SHARING SECRET

It was never mentioned anywhere. It wasn't that it was in any way important but not ever mentioning things could have its advantages.

A couple of years back, when Elizabeth's husband Henry, The school's Principal, mentioned to his wife that one of the applicants for the positions of Secretary to the Principal was an ex-private girls-school student who had attended the same school as Elizabeth, she immediately set about making sure the woman got the job.

Wives can be good at that sort of thing.

Henry's new secretary, Sandra Goodchild had been at Tonbridge Wells Girls Grammar School a couple of years after Elizabeth but they soon discovered that their experiences had been very similar, especially with regard to discipline.

One of the smaller private girls schools near the Sussex border, in Kent, the school followed a long tradition regarding discipline.

Flagellation or *pursuing the path of penance* as it was referred to, was a regular occurrence at the school. So endemic was it that, "The Art" was practiced, not only by the staff on the senior girls, but the senior girls themselves would administer it to each other and to a select few of the staff as well, always in secret of course.

Strappings, spankings and whippings were a major topic of conversation. Everything at school rotated around who had what done to them, or what they had done to someone else.

So popular was this pastime that it would seem to have been the foremost form of entertainment for the hormonally charged scholars, and quite naturally, girlfriends looked after one another after such events, tending each other's discomfort with soothing balms and very loving words.

It was over tea and biscuits one day, a year or more after Sandra started work at the school that she and Elizabeth had 'the conversation' meaning telling each other about their disciplinary experiences.

Far from seeing what happened as shocking, both women happily recounted their most memorable experiences enjoying the camaraderie that sharing can bring about.

"So, Miss Fulbright was still there, I assume? Was she still active with the students backsides?"

Sandra giggled. "You bet she was. Probably you were calling a very red glowing bum "a Fulbright" as were we."

"Oh yes! I was lucky to never be caught being naughty enough to cop one. What about you?"

Sandra made a face and gritted her teeth.

"I did earn a Fulbright once even though I wasn't technically guilty. But as you would know, the old bat never missed an opportunity and that voice and tone as she was about to start, *This hurts me far more than it hurts you young lady. But its for your own good*." God, I hated that woman."

Elizabeth stared at her new friend and smiled.

"And did you get loving attention from your friends afterwards, Sandra?"

Sandra's face turned a little pink.

"Yes, I did, Elizabeth," then she smiled. "It almost made it worth it."

They chatted on, reliving those faraway days. Then Elizabeth asked if Sandra had owned a Spider.

Again, the woman coloured up.

"I still do, darling. Wouldn't go anywhere without it. How about you?"

It was Elizabeth's turn to show a little colour in her face although it was probably from excitement rather than embarrassment and in a hushed voice she replied, "Couldn't live without it! I might not use it often but I want to know its close at hand if and when I want to use it."

The two fell silent, each staring at the other, both aware that they were close to entering an as yet unexplored area of intimacy. Then Sandra spoke.

"You don't have anyone who ..."

Elizabeth replied before Sandra could finish.

"No, I don't. Would you be interested? My husband goes away once a month for a couple of days and I'm alone in a very big house, Maybe you ..."

"Yes, Elizabeth, I would love to. It's a long time since I attended to anyone but myself, but if you are prepared to try, I'd love to be your Miss Muffet and for you to be mine."

The two women smiled lovingly at one another.

Although Sandra, with Elizabeth's knowledge and tacit approval, was now also enjoying Elizabeth's husband's new found mojo, neither had reached out to each other in an intimate way. But that was about to change.

Elizabeth moved closer and put her arms out in a welcoming gesture and Sandra responded immediately, joining her in a hug of complicit understanding.

"Yes, Sandra? Let us be consenting Miss Muffet's'. I would love that," Elizabeth whispered.

Then they stared into each others eyes and without further consideration, their lips made contact and they enjoyed a first tentative kiss, slowly at first, but then, to enjoy this first moment more energetically, they thrust their tongues into each others mouths.

Both were enjoying the moment and contemplating whether to take things further and slip their hands into intimate places, but then the door opened and Henry Philips walked in.

Henry observed the kissing women and smiled, avoiding asking about whatever it was that brought the two together.

"My goodness, I'm in time for tea and biscuits. How splendid; whats news? Life is just going on as normal I see?"

Irony was Henry's speciality.

Elizabeth and Sandra parted and laughed and looked at each other with new interest.

"Same old, darling. Sandra and I were just celebrating your new manly presence around the place. It seems quickies might now be appearing on the menu. Well done, darling. It's a welcome sign of your good health."

In the highly charged world of the young women at TWIGGS, discipline took different forms, depending on who was doing what to whom.

It was common knowledge that the highly personal nature of exposing oneself to discipline could be exciting. Disciplining each other was nevertheless, sustained by very strong rules. But within the rules, enterprising young women worked out enjoyable routines to make "*pursuing the path of penance*" experience a much loved pastime.

Spanking with a bare hand was allowed so long as the hand was flat and only came into contact with a buttock. No finger movement allowed.

Self-flagellation with a Spider was probably the favourite pastime. A spider was the name given to a little eight chord flagellating instrument which was available from a certain senior student who in turn, procured their stock from a staff member, almost certainly the afore-mentioned Miss Fulbright.

A good Spider sported thin leather strands like were once used in mens work boots, each one knotted near the end. The handle just happened to be smooth with a rounded knob at the end and long enough that some might find it useful for other purposes. There were cheaper models available.

Students enjoyed being attended to by a friend, commonly referred to as their Miss Muffet, but the handiness of the little flagellator was that it could be used alone, comfortably reaching ones buttocks and easy to flick between the legs from either the front or the back.

A Spider could inflict a heavy stinging sensation without cutting into the flesh, and the strong searing tingling sensations that ensued were much appreciated and often accompanied by full or partial orgasms.

The rules forbade touching either by the appointed Miss Muffet or anyone else present; not even the recipient of the flogging was allowed to touch herself.

In keeping with tradition, the rules forbade that this activity was ever to be confused with a sexual one, despite the powerful erotic motivation of most encounters.

The young women loved it, and often overlooked the rules. But then everyone has their secrets.

NINE
SPIDER WOMEN UNITE

It was Henry Nichols weekend away with his golfing mates and Elizabeth was excited about her planned first get together with Henry's secretary, the beautiful Sandra.

Elizabeth and Sandra had told each other about their experiences at their old school – Tonbridge Wells Girls Grammar in England – in particular, those things relating to discipline.

Both women had cautiously and excitedly exposed themselves to each other's views on the art of *pursuing the path of penance* and they knew that they wanted to revisit those adolescent moments with a similarly experienced friend. Each had agreed it would be with each other.

"Welcome! Drop your bag down just there. The kettle is on and we can relax. We have the place to ourselves for the whole weekend if needs be."

Sandra laughed. "Who knows? We might fail miserably to rekindle that special TWGGS spirit and you send me home early."

Elizabeth looked at the delightful slightly younger woman. "I think that whatever happens, we will find something to enjoy together, Sandra. Even if it is only exercising in the basement gym."

Sandra giggled. "I can't wait to get excited on the leg extension machine, or feel the sensations one can experience between the legs on the stationary bicycle."

The banter continued as two slightly nervous women contemplated the moment when they would confront each other as the other's Miss Muffet.

Eventually, two highly excited women, each carrying a small case, descended the few steps to the basement. The gym had been there when Henry and Elizabeth bought the house and they figured it could stay and that they might use it someday.

The two stopped just inside the little rest room and Elizabeth put down her case and turned to Sandra.

"I've been thinking about how this will work, darling, and as we are now much older, I suggest we both should add to the experience by stripping first and doing things in the nude.

"The old rules need not apply exactly, and I'm sure we would appreciate the greater freedom it would give us to do the things we really want to do. Are you happy with that idea, Sandra?"

Sandra moved closer to Elizabeth and stared into her eyes and smiled.

"I totally agree, darling. Lets get naked."

Two nude beauties unpacked their little cases and showed each other their Spiders, giggling and furtively swishing them around. Then, as arranged earlier by tossing a coin, Elizabeth went first and stood facing the wall.

"I'm ready, Sandra."

Sandra stared at the naked vision standing in front of her and memories of her school days flooded back. Then she prepared herself.

"Coming for you now."

Two exhausted but happy women lay on the restroom mattress, both still in a sort of hypnotic state. Their eyes were glazed and they had both orgasmed more times than they could remember.

And still, each one came whenever the other began to apply soothing balm; and they no longer tried to hide the sounds they made. Their earlier screams were far more significant than those magic utterances they made now, when each touched the others hot tingling buttocks.

Eventually, following a considerable silence, Elizabeth's little voice mumbled. "Splendid!" Then Sandra croaked a "Hear, hear!"

A further few minutes of quiet reflection. Then Elizabeth spoke.

"If you are still happy to stay the night, Sandra, we can …" at which point Sandra finished her sentence for her,

" … do it all over again? Yes, Elizabeth! Yes, please!"

The TWIGG's tradition lives on, albeit with some adult modifications.

TEN

A NEW TWIGGS GIRL

Henry was in a long conversation with another man about the maintenance of sporting venues, in particular, grass types and the fight against intrusive species. It was in this not exactly exciting moment that Elizabeth received a text from Sandra, elsewhere in the building.

Just met a Twiggs old-girl. Find us in second alcove after piano.
Please come now or text.

Elizabeth texted *'on my way'* and excused herself, saying that Sandra needed her and she would meet up with Henry again in a little while.

Meeting another girl who attended her old school in Kent was going to be exciting. Sandra was the only one Elizabeth knew in Australia so this could be a momentous occasion.

Elizabeth entered the alcove not knowing what to expect. After so many years, people might very likely have changed from their school days persona. Life away from the safety of their old school had definitely changed both her and Sandra.

Sandra sat in an arm chair and a very large woman wearing a big smile sat opposite on the sofa along with a thin younger woman, close beside her.

Sandra introduced Elizabeth.

"Elizabeth? I'd like you to meet Margret Thornycroft and her partner Meg Musgrave.

"Margret was at Twiggs a couple of years before you. She was as excited as I was to meet a fellow Twiggian. Now she's met two, all in the same day!"

Elizabeth smiled warmly at the two woman.

"Pleased to meet you both. And yes, Twiggian's are a rarity, especially here in Australia. So where do you live? Are you both Sydney based?"

"We are in the Blue Mountains, about two and half hours drive from here. I have a Welsh Cob stud and riding school and provide Eco friendly accomodation.

"I purchased an already established horse property and added twenty self service units.

"I bred Cobs in Wales for many years, but after a visit to Australia around ten years ago, I discovered that this is where I belonged. I put a deposit on the Blue Mountains farm and went home and sold the business I had, exporting my six finest Cobs to the new place in Australia. I've never looked back and now employ four people full time. Best decision I ever made."

Both Elizabeth and Sandra were in love with Margret's delightful private school and slightly haughty mannish voice. She epitomised those Twiggs girls who spent most of their time in jodhpurs and only talked about horses and fox hunting.

Margret's attire was the classic private school outfit with just a bit of butch detail. A hacking jacket with leather patches on the elbows and around the sleeve edges. A plain cream shirt and a tie sporting a horseshoe tie pin. A tweed skirt looked as though it fitted closely over her extra large rear and thighs. Thick tan stockings and sensible lace-up brown brogues completed the picture.

"Now while it is lovely talking to you both, Meg and I must get back to the farm. Pity we can't wait for the wedding party."

Margret slipped a hand into a jacket fob pocket and produced a card and offered it to Sandra.

"It has been lovely meeting you and we would love to spend more time with the both of you. Here is my card. I'm offering you both three free nights at Fine Q Lodge. Please say you will come. We Twiggs girls have much to share and I'm sure you would be happy to share lots of things with the two of us."

Margret's smile showed just a hint of possible complicity, indicating her interest in discovering Sandra and Elizabeth's relationship details and gender proclivities.

As the two rose to leave, Margret turned and looked back over her shoulder and smiled, almost mischievously.

"If you haven't already noticed, you will discover that I have much to offer a fully experienced Twiggian. There are things I've missed over the years. Who knows? You might be able to fix that for me?

And you will also love meeting some of our regulars, all of whom can bring something different into your life. Call me soon and I'll fit you in."

———————

When Elizabeth and Sandra were alone again, they agreed that for whatever reason, the offer sounded heartfelt and exciting.

"Are you thinking what I'm thinking, darling?"

"Probably, Sandra? She was obviously referring to that special something we've rediscovered.

Given Margret's size, we would need two Spiders?"

"At the one time, I suspect, Elizabeth. They say that big is better. I'm prepared to think that from what a saw of Margret's backside, it simply couldn't be any better."

"You're quite right, darling. We could be her two Miss Muffet's. It could give new meaning to caring and sharing."

Now darling. I'm getting excited. Henry's been asked to travel away this weekend to speak at a two-day seminar. I wonder if I could …"

" … find a willing Miss Muffet? Yes, darling. I know one who would jump at the chance to help you out."

ELEVEN

HOLY ORDERS

Percival Lemon managed to leave his diocese before he was defrocked following complaints about his behaviour with a parishioner.

Knowing things were not going his way, he left the church before they could get rid of him.

Mr Lemon kept very much to himself except for his flock of devoted and loving ladies who didn't want to give him up and who he continued to visit regularly.

More than a dozen women enjoyed his company on a regular basis, replying to his text messages "Lemons on Tuesday 2pm?" or whatever regular day they enjoyed his attention. "Yes, please," was their usual reply, sometime they added the name they most often addressed him with; "Yes please, Father," or "Yes please, Percy."

Over the years, Percy's pastoral care had morphed into a sexual care model. After all, he figured, love was supposed to be universal and without shame.

As it happened, when Percy could no longer live in the manse, he went in search of a modest affordable house and discovered his dream home, a little weatherboard cottage with three mature and prolific lemon trees in an orchard that covered most of the back garden.

So Percy did bring lemons to his flock. Always arriving with a shopping bag of fruit; he sometimes brought pears or peaches or whatever was in season.

'Squeezing a lemon' became a fun euphemism amongst his flock for squeezing or playing with Percy's private parts.

The great success of Percy's sexual adventures with his flock was most likely due to his measured and thoughtful approach to the women who enjoyed him. He was never in a hurry and was happy to give more than he received. And he was good at judging their moods. He also responded to them as people and not simply as sexual objects.

Percy's flock covered a wide range of ages.

Ruby was the oldest at 72, the wife of his friend, the late Reverend Russell, a sandy haired firebrand C of E vicar who always admonished Percy for being in the Popes army. His dying friend's request was for Percy to "Look after Ruby. She's got a soft spot for you," accompanied by a nudge and a wink.

And Ruby did have a soft spot for Percy. Ruby was a neat little thing, very active and quaint.

After she had poured his tea, Ruby would move her kitchen chair around to be close to Percy's, then, after making sure Percy was holding his chocolate biscuit, she proceeded to undo his trousers and feel around for his cock, all the while calling out in a gentle voice, "I know you're there, Mr Lemon. I'm waiting. Come out and be squeezed."

Once she had Percy's cock in her hand, she would excitedly rub, fondle, lick and suck it, while all the times talking to it, even telling it rude stories about her youth. She seemed to enjoy reliving those moments and Percy enjoyed listening.

"Ruby's got a soft spot for you. Are you ready?" And then she would look up into Percy's eyes waiting for him to nod in the affirmative.

Once Percy had finished his biscuit, Ruby would stand up and remove her knickers and in her thick blue stockings and little heels, straddle him, feeding him into her soft spot.

Then Ruby would ride him, laughing and gurgling and talking loudly about all the rude fun things she did with boys when she was young and before her husband had appeared and saved her soul.

"Oh, how the boys loved to fuck me, Percy. What is that term they use nowadays? I know! I was a cum bucket and was hardly ever without something in there to keep me happy.

"And it wasn't just the young ones, Percy. I had it off with half the men in the town.

The baker would give me donuts after he'd buried himself in my special spot, and the butcher's delivery man would leave me a pair of rabbits for my mum if I wanked him and sucked is cock.

"I could pop into the cabinetmakers workshop whenever I felt like it and when I heard him working and he'd give it to me bent over his work stool and amid the resin scented pine shavings that covered the floor. I loved it!

"Even the vicar enjoyed my favours. He would ask me to visit the church to help with the flowers, then when the other helpers had left, he'd take me out to the vestry and tell me to get onto my knees to pray.

"Then he would pull up his cassock and wave his big cock at me, knowing full well that I would want it. Then he made me bend over while he put lavender oil on my bum then he would make me hold his cock and help him stick it in where he normally stuck it with one of the choir boys.

"I soon got to like it and made certain I was always there on the day the ladies changed the flowers.

"But then the Reverend Russell arrived as the new vicar. Once he discovered how happy I could make him, he got very possessive and insisted that we get married, thinking that would curb my activities. But I still managed to get it elsewhere whenever I felt like it.

"I'm so lucky I've got you Percy. Oh and George over the road although it's getting too hard to get him up these days. But he feels me up nicely so I should be grateful.

"I do miss those days but at least I've got a good memory. And I've got you, you lovely man. Now, have you got something for a horny old lady, Percy? My bucket needs topping up with something wet and warm."

———

Then there were the identical twins, Paula and Primrose, aged in their late forties.

If there was ever a mystery that intrigued Percy more than the mystery of the Holy Ghost, Primrose was it.

Primrose, the youngest by only two or three hours, was mentally and physically tuned to things that her sister did.

When Percy was making love to the older Paula on the big double bed, and Primrose was siting back in just her undies awaiting her turn, Percy was fascinated to see the younger sister orgasm at the same moment that Paula threw herself up at him, screaming as she came.

He noted that when this happened, Primrose was not touching herself between her legs nor caressing her breasts. She just came at the same instant as her sister, as if she was the one enjoying Percy's cock.

Percy Lemon had read about this phenomena over the years. It came up in writings about witchcraft. And asylums had their share of identical twins incarcerated in their huge Victorian institutions in years gone bye.

It wasn't just a sexual thing he was observing in Primrose. In conversations with the two it seemed that she also experienced pain if her sister cut herself or fell over or banged her head on the low door-ways in their cottage.

Percy never stopped wondering about the girl's seemingly improb-able reactions to her sisters feelings. Over time, he worked out that the intensity of Paula's feelings governed the responses from Primrose.

He noted that when Primrose watched as her sister sucked Percy's cock, she showed no sign of feeling anything until the moment when Paula sensed that Percy was about to come and increased her attention.

Then, as he erupted, Primrose, threw herself about in an orgasmic response leaving Percy wondering what her sister Paula must have felt at the moment he ejaculated.

Primrose loved being shagged and lovingly kissed and she loved to fondle Percy's testicles. She was quick to orgasm, thanking him after-wards and refusing to let him remove himself from her until she was ready.

Her sister Paula loved watching them shagging, playing with herself so that she could join them in the final moments. But there was never a sign that she directly felt things the way her sister Primrose felt them.

Primrose often finished her sisters sentences and Paula never complained. This too, depended on the intensity of Paula's mindset as she spoke.

It remained a mystery for Percy Lemon, but one that, in the end, he was happy to just let be. Having them both was a delight he would never tire of.

―――

Polly was a big lady. Her chest was super-sized and her huge back-side protruded equally in the opposite direction.

She had never married even though she had a pretty face and a delightful smile.

Polly first invited the priest home some years back to visit her sick mother who died shortly after Father Lemon's visit. Then Polly contacted him again and asked him to visit so that she could thank him for his kindness to her mother.

After the obligatory tea and biscuit and listening to Polly's tale of woe about being too big to get a husband, and Percy's rash statement that a man would be a fool to 'pass up such a beautiful woman', the big lady reached over and hungrily groped under his cassock, finding his ever willing member already in the early stages of a serious stand.

"Please, Father. You must do the right thing by my lonely body?" she cried.

Then Polly took him by the hand and led him to the kitchen table. She removed her knickers and lay face down over the edge, then she lifted her skirt, displaying the biggest and most beautiful and flawless backside that Percy had ever seen; and before he could even begin to work out where to start, Polly had dragged his penis to her mass of wet curls and slid him into her vagina, screaming "thank you father".

The image of Polly's lavish arse atop legs which quickly slimmed down to tiny ankles and feet, put Percy in mind of the Harvest Festival celebrations of his youth.

Percy imagined Polly's rear on display amidst giant pumpkins and squashes and other cucurbits and vegetables in the main produce tent at the annual village fair.

Polly's giant backside was the centrepiece, like a shrine, and like a shrine, everyone unwittingly rubbed a smooth buttock for luck as they passed bye, commenting that, 'it must have taken a lot of effort to grow this one'.

"I'm in need of pastoral care, Father. Please don't disappoint me," Polly would call out each time he arrived

Over the regular monthly visits that followed, Percy Lemon enjoyed Polly on the kitchen table and on the carpet, while the huge energetic woman screamed and laughed and begged for more.

And one day, when Percy reached for the butter dish and dabbed her anus with fat, she screamed in fear but then once he'd introduced his cock to that other palace of enjoyment, Polly would never let him leave the house without a good dose of what she called "bum loving".

Only months following Polly's initiation, and at Percy's suggestion, Polly spread her wings and very soon she was entertaining other men on a regular basis, ensuring, of course that the butter dish was always at hand.

Be it a delivery man, the meter reader, a tradesman, a salesman or an itinerant looking for work, Polly would offer then her tale of woe about being unable to find a mate because of her size. And her sad tale never failed.

Hardly a day passed that Polly wasn't lying spreadeagled over the kitchen table enjoying the attention of an energetic admirer and experiencing the pleasures that should naturally attend such a magnificent derriere.

Polly managed to satisfy all of her places of pleasure, always remembering that Father Lemmon had given her the necessary blessing.

And of course, Percy would always be around each month with lemons, and he would never leave without enjoying his "bum loving" big girl.

TWELVE

CATCHING UP AT LAST!

"That was Gerald on the phone, darling. He asked if he could come over. He said something had happened and would it be all right if he stayed the night. I told him he would be most welcome."

"Did he give any details of what had happened, Margo?"

"Yes, Andrea, he did. He said that Glenyce had left him. Apparently she'd met two brothers late on the night of the wedding reception. They offered her a granny flat at the back of their place.

"She told him that she wasn't coming back and would he go somewhere for a couple of days while she moved her stuff out."

Andrea stared at Margo as they both thought about the implications for their friend and what this might all mean for him and for them.

"He will need gentle support, darling. Now that he knows about us and seems comfortable with it, that should make it much easier."

It was quite late when Gerald arrived. He didn't seem at all dispirited or upset.

"I'm actually relieved that she's at last out of my life," Gerald said, smiling as he helped himself to another chocolate biscuit.

"I've been thinking a lot lately about my life and seeing how you two have made such big changes. I've been able to start thinking about things I might want instead of constantly thinking about keeping Glenyce happy."

Andrea and Margo looked at Gerald and then at each other.

"And have you thought enough about things that you now know what you would like, Gerald?"

Gerald blushed just a little. "Actually, yes I have. You've both been an inspiration and I now know that I want a lot more of what you two are getting from each other."

His friends both laughed. Then Andrea remarked that if he was referring to what she thought he was referring to, she had the answer.

Margo and Gerald looked at Andrea, wondering just what she would say next.

"You turned forty last month, Gerald. You are now old enough to join the Swingers Club. It's a younger age for men. Margo and I have recently joined. We turned forty-five which is when women are eligible for membership."

Margo and Gerald continued to stare at Andrea.

"I guess that would be a good place to start. Yes, what a good idea, Andrea. I'll join up and see if I can get lucky."

Everyone laughed and relaxed. Then Margo glanced at Andrea before she ventured her response.

"Would getting lucky mean you would be looking for a new relationship, Gerald? You don't think it might be a bit soon for that?"

Gerald laughed out loud. "Hell no! I just want sex. A bit of loving along the way would be okay, I suppose."

Margo and Andrea looked at each other, thinking the same thoughts.

"Lets go and put on our pyjamas, Margo and then sit in the in front of the fire in the lounge where it's more comfortable. You've given us a lot to think about, Gerald.

"Our friendship is important and we don't want to see you getting dragged off by some mad woman, do we Margo?"

As they wandered out of the kitchen, Gerald laughingly remarked that even a mad woman might be a good short term answer.

"Did you bring pyjama's, Gerald?"

"Yes, I did. I'll go and put them on."

———————

"What do think Margo? Will he come around to seeing us as potential lovers? Or will he keep seeing us as just friends?"

Margo sat on the bed buttoning up her new pyjama top as Andrea slipped out of her knickers then pulled on her new shorty pyjama pants.

"Bingo! I've just worked it out, Andrea. I don't know why we didn't think of it before."

Margo stood up and came over and hugged her lover.

"What is it, Margo? What have you worked out."

"It's the bloke thing. Single mindedness. Gerald sees us a couple and men don't interfere with couples. Well, at least, not in front of each other. They will often act differently if the husband is elsewhere.

"Gerald sees us both as being unavailable because we are a couple."

So where does that leave us, Margo?

Margo looked at her lover with excitement in her eyes.

"If we want him to do anything, we must see him one at a time; never as a couple. I think a level of intimacy would be possible if we saw him individually."

Andrea gasped. "I believe you might be right, darling. He's treating us as sort of a husband and wife couple. Why didn't we see it before?"

"Because we are women. Firstly, women don't look for sexual encounter potential overtly. Well, not usually, as far as I remember. And despite what their husband might assume, their wives are to smart to want to jeopardise their relationship.

"Also, they are more open to each other anyway or if they are not, they soon indicate their intentions."

"So if we are right about this, my love, we need to approach him separately. We must recreate the good old fashioned boy meets girl situation.

"The only problem now is deciding who will be first. And not only that, he might think we are cheating on each other. Gosh! Getting up close and dirty with a man can be so complicated."

Andrea laughed, saying it better all be worth it. "And I hope he finds out how much trouble he's been."

"We need to tell him up front on our first move. Yes! That's it! Tell him that we are both interested but thought it best to approach him separately."

"I think you are right, Margot. So lets do it before he falls asleep."

Margo smiled at her true love.

"I think you should go first. You be the first slut off the rank. I'll wait and do my slut thing when the time comes.

"Just pop on some lippy and get your sexy self in there. And you have my permission and blessings to go berserk."

Andrea laughed and grabbed Margot and kissed her.

"Okay, sweetheart. Wish me luck and fingers crossed."

Andrea began to leave but then she stopped and turned to face Margo.

"Darling? This does feel a little strange. Its like I'm heading off to cheat on you. Why am feeling like this?"

Margo moved over and put her arms around her and they nuzzled their faces into each others necks. The two remained silent.

"I think we can get confused easily. If we were both at the Swingers Club being chatted up my men or women, we wouldn't have this problem, would we?

"We would regard everything that happened there as simply a 'casual encounter'.

"I can only suggest that we make a pact right now that we see ourselves and each other as simply taking our bodies for a nice walk.

"Also that we know that we will share with each other all that happens just as if we were doing it together. In fact the only reason we aren't doing it together is so that it is easier for Gerald to cope.

"If all goes well and we both have a moment with him, he should very quickly accept that whether he's with one or both of us, for us it is all okay."

Andrea let go of Margo, who laughed and felt reassured.

"I think I'll go and cut up some fruit. I'll bring you some but if I don't, it means I got lucky."

———

Andrea stood at the bench in her bare feet and her new silk shorty pyjamas, cutting up pears and an orange when Gerald came into the kitchen. He was busy towelling his black curly hair.

"Good evening, Andrea," he called. "You've got a great shower. I feel so invigorated."

Andrea turned and smiled at him and glanced down at the front of Gerald's stripey fleecy pyjamas. There was a bulge suggesting that something was pushing against the fabric.

"Hi, Gerald. You do look invigorated."

Andrea smiled at him and lowered her eyes to indicate what she was referring to.

Gerald seemed not to notice. He came up behind her and reached around her to steal a piece of pear.

Andrea realised that whatever was looking for a way out of Gerald's pyjama pants, was gently pushing against her backside but she couldn't be sure that Gerald was aware of it. This was a moment that Andrea decided she should take advantage off.

Andrea gently pushed her backside back until she could feel Gerald's object of interest hard up against her bum. Then she took a risk and began to make tiny gyrating movements against him and she heard Gerald gasp.

"Andrea? You are being naughty and … "

Andrea didn't let him finish.

"It feels really good to me, Gerald. Would you prefer that I stopped."

"No, don't! Keep doing it, Andrea. Your backside feels wonderful."

Andrea immediately pushed back a little harder, noticing that

Gerald's cock had suddenly increased in size and was now rubbing up and down between her cheeks.

"Oh, Gerald. You feel so good. Can I turn around, darling? I want to see what your secret is? Pretty please?"

Gerald moved back slightly and Andrea turned and put her hands around his neck and kissed him passionately.

"It's okay, Gerald. Margo and I are both hungry for you," she whispered.

Then Andrea slid to the floor and took Gerald's large member out of his pyjama's and in moments had the bulbous shiny head between her lips. Then she began to suck him, hearing him groan and feeling his hand on the top of her head.

Andrea let him go and stood up and took his hand and lead Gerald into the lounge and drew him down onto the sofa and knelt beside him and renewed her sucking activities.

Andrea's eyes were closed as she moved into a beautiful meditative moment of cock sucking and not thinking of anything else.

Then she felt Gerald's fingers exploring inside her pyjama leg, and then he was fingering her wet pussy and she let go of his cock.

"Yes, Gerald, yes, my darling. Play with my pussy, please."

Then she felt his hands pulling down her pyjamas. Then he pushed open her legs.

"Let me fuck you, Andrea. I've always wanted to."

"Oh yes, Gerald, but you must promise to fuck our darling Margo, too? You must know that she wants you too. And we are offering ourselves as a package deal to do whatever you want with."

Gerald laughed as he manoeuvred their bodies into a comfortable position on the sofa.

"Yes, of course I will. I will want to fuck both of you, every day and forever."

Andrea, replied quickly, not wanting to put him off his stroke. "And we will often want you to have us both together, too."

At that moment, Gerald planted his cock firmly in Andrea's cunt. She called out and she gasped. Then she tuned in to his solidly rhythmic shagging mode and the two went to heaven.

"Oh yes, Gerald, that is heavenly." Andrea gasped. "At last, you darling man."

Andrea carried a bowl of fruit into the bedroom. Margo was asleep, so she left the fruit beside the bed. But as she was about to leave, the sleeping woman awoke.

"Don't go darling. Did things go well with you and Gerald?"

Andrea went and sat on the bed and smiled down at her true love.

"Very well, darling. Would you like to check the evidence? I'll hop in beside you and let you investigate. There just could be something there you'd like to lick up."

Margo came alive.

"Oh, you slut, you. Quick! Get in and open your legs. I'll start there. Then I'll try the fruit."

THIRTEEN

BEATRICE BACK WHERE SHE STARTED

A month or more had passed before Beatrice heard from Penelope. She assumed she and Heath had travelled away but wasn't sure about the circumstances.

When Penny called and asked if she could come over, Beatrice was relieved to hear her voice.

"Of course, darling. Come soon."

Hearing the story of what happened at the wedding was better than a novel or a television soapy.

Olga ran off with Leonid to begin with, and Heath and Penny married later in the day in the same church and with the same preacher.

"Before I forget, Bea, I'm here to invite you to celebrate our marriage properly at a party next week.

"We haven't invited many who were at the first wedding party, just a few people we would like to share our good news with and who we feel deserve an explanation for what happened.

"By the way, we've invited Sandra so you won't be alone."

Penny gave a knowing smile.

"And Elizabeth?"

"No! She and Henry are holidaying somewhere and won't be back in time."

Beatrice thanked her then told Penny how well she looked.

"Being married is obviously good for you, Penny. Or is it just all that fresh air from your honeymoon?"

Penny coloured up. "Lets just say that Heath is looking after me very well."

"So where will the party be, Penny. You won't need a large venue, I imagine?"

"Well, funny as it may sound, we will be at the same venue as last time. Ursula offered us a special price. The only thing is that, like last time, we'll be there on the regular Swingers Club night. Apparently they are quite happy to share."

Penny looked at Beatrice oddly. "Some people stayed on and enjoyed themselves with the Swingers, I hear. But I don't have any names."

It was Beatrice's turn to colour up.

"Well, they would have had to fill in time in case you suddenly appeared, I suppose."

Both women laughed.

"And tell me, what happened to Leonid? Is he still around?"

"Heavens no! Olga who wasn't Olga but really Maria Dziirava, took him to a huge yacht moored at Central Quay close to that big motel there.

"The boat was called Thalia, and it was owned by a Russian Oligarch.

"It turns out that the Russian mafia wanted Leonid in relation to a scam organised by him and his mother among London's expat Russian community.

"I don't know what happened to him after that. I don't want to know, actually."

Beatrice was impressed with how her young friend had changed. She had matured and Beatrice figured that much of it might be attributed to her new husbands loving attention.

"Well, that would be nice, but Sandra and I will enjoy ourselves, I'm sure. She and I had a great time at your last wedding.

The two women laughed and kissed and said their goodbye's.

"Oh and Penny, if you need help with anything, just ask. You know? Getting me to watch out for anyone that you'd prefer wasn't there?"

Penny laughed. "I think this time, Bea, you can just lay back and enjoy yourself."

The two laughed at Penny alluding to Beatrice's previous Swinger Club activities.

"I definitely will, darling."

Sandra was excited when Beatrice called her.

"It just wouldn't be the same without you, darling. I need someone to get into trouble with and who better than you."

The two chatted, savouring the moments they remembered enjoying together with members of the Swingers Club.

"We might just get lucky again, darling. I wonder how slutty we can dress without looking over the top."

"I'm sure we can hide our charms a little bit for the wedding part. After that, it might become a 'whose the sluttiest slut' competition."

Beatrice was surprise when Penny called to ask if she could come over. It was only a few days after her previous visit.

"Well, Penny. This is a surprise. Am I in for a shock?"

Penny looked lovingly at Beatrice and smiled.

"You might be."

The two settled back on the sofa in front of Beatrice's much loved log fire. Penny reached out and took her hand.

"There is something I wanted to tell you earlier, but I put it off. Now I do need to tell you."

Beatrice sensed that this was a moment to be serious, and refrained from making a quip.

"Heath has recently had problems with his prostate and is having tests. He is worried and he has told me that things might have to change. He says that he may no longer be able to provide the same loving attention that we have enjoyed so far in our relationship."

Beatrice squeezed Penny's hand.

"I'm so sorry, darling. That is not good news."

"Heath has told me that he would like me to enjoy other people, to compensate for his likely lack of physical attention. I told him he was being silly but he insisted that we look at changing things.

"He thinks I should explore bisexual options, saying that from what he has observed, women with women are mostly very good together.

"I told him he was talking nonsense, but then he said that he had arranged for me to spend a few days with his younger sister, Lena, at her horse stud near Bowral. Lena is a lesbian who has recently gone through a separation, and she could do with a bit of help on the farm.

"I couldn't find a way to talk him out of it so I leave next Wednesday."

Penny stared at Beatrice who was wondering what was coming next.

"I thought that of the few swinging people I know, you would be my choice to teach me how to be with a woman, Beatrice. Please say you will help me?"

Beatrice was shocked and she needed to sort out her thoughts. She realised that Penny was stressed and needed reassurance that the heavens were not about to fall in on her.

"Darling? Being bye is not a big deal. Kissing a woman instead of a man can get you to the same places. I'm not sure that you need to know much more than that. Kissing is the key to everything, whatever your preferences are."

Beatrice was now looking more closely at Penny. The neatly dressed slender young woman was very attractive. It was just that Beatrice had never looked at her in a sexual way before.

"In that case, Beatrice, maybe if you just kissed me then I would feel as though I had made the first step."

Beatrice listened before answering.

"Well, Penny. The truth is that if I kissed you in the way bisexual women kiss, I might not want to stop, if you know what I mean. You are a very attractive young lady."

Penny was looking at Beatrice, but now with a glint in her eye, and her smile widened.

"I'd love you to kiss me, Beatrice. And whatever you want to do, please just do it."

Beatrice waited a moment to try to consider all things but the look on Penny's face told her that the young woman had already made her decision and was anticipating Beatrice's next move.

As Beatrice reached out her arms towards Penny, she murmured that Penny was very beautiful. Then she put her lips on Penny's lips and the young woman responded by instantly pushing her tongue into Beatrice's mouth as she wrapped her arms around her and pulled her close.

The two women clung to each other. Then Penny pulled herself away and looked into Beatrice's eyes.

"Do whatever you want to me darling. I think I'm going to love whatever you ask me for. Can I touch your breasts?"

Beatrice listened, then she unbuttoned her top so that Penny could see her cleavage. Then she moved one of Penny's hand and pushed her fingers down into a bra cup, feeling and hearing the young woman moan as she discovered a nipple.

"Oh Beatrice, don't stop, please don't stop."

Then Beatrice unbuttoned Penny's top and dragged down her bra, exposing her small breasts. Then she too, fingered a nipple.

Penny was moaning and breathing deeply when Beatrice informed her that she was about to remove Penny's knickers.

Penny wriggled and gasped, then she pushed herself down into the settee and stretched the lower part of her body out while Beatrice lifted her skirt and looked down on her stay-up white stockings and her lacy pants.

"God, you are so beautiful, Penny. How could anyone not want to fuck you?"

"Oh, yes please, Bea. Please?

Beatrice methodically removed Penny's shirt and bra, then she eased the woman's knickers down over her knees and feet and tossed them away. Then she stared at Penny's almost hairless pussy before reaching up and kissed Penny on the lips.

"Are you comfortable, darling? I'm going to lick and suck your special place, but first I will remove some of my clothes. Touch me wherever you want, darling."

———

Over the next little while, two new lovers enjoyed the rhapsody of mingling their body parts with their fingers and tongues. Both woman screamed and orgasmed and both women gave thanks for their coming together.

———

Sometimes Beatrice thought about going to the Cactus Club with girl friends. But since she and Sandra had enjoyed themselves with two men they met at the wedding reception's Swingers Club later in the evening, picking up someone at the Cactus Club had lost its appeal.

Beatrice had experienced real men that night, and now she couldn't go back to the hit-and-miss roulette wheel of a rumble at the Willing Wall with men that most times were not sober enough to appreciate what was on offer.

Beatrice wanted more.

When Beatrice told Sandra on the phone about how she was feeling and not wanting to go clubbing, Sandra commiserated with her. But then she told Beatrice that she had news which might bring them both some excitement.

"I had a phone call yesterday from a woman who will be attending Penny and Heath's wedding.

"Penny had given her the list of who she had invited after the woman, whose name is Susannah, said she would happily organise a small group of those attendees interested, to better enjoy themselves at the Swingers Club later in the evening.

"At first, I was not especially interested thinking that you and I were pretty good at sorting out our own agenda. But then she mentioned her friend Megan and I suddenly remembered that Arnold and Ray had mentioned those two names when they said how their wives would love to meet us.

"I was suddenly interested. The upshot is that I've agreed that you and I will join their party. I hope you don't mind, Bea, but we did agree that those guys were really very good. And Susannah sounded like she knew her way around, too.

Beatrice laughed and said how she now understood why Sandra was such a wonderful secretary to the Principal.

"I'm in your hands, darling. Or in any hands you wish to put me in. Love you. Sleep tight!"

————

Beatrice put on her warm pyjamas and went to bed, hoping she would have her favourite dream.

In her dream, Beatrice would be making love to more than one person.

Beatrice could never see her lovers face's in the dream, nor could she be sure how many there were. Sometimes it was a man with a respectable stiffy; at other moments it was a woman, begging Beatrice to suck her giant clit. Whichever way it went, Beatrice would wake up, exhausted and happy and when she checked, she was also very wet.

Life was good.

AFTERWORD

In a matriarchal structure, such as exists in some tribes in South India, women have natural confidence in their own womanhood. They know their importance and that they are different from men in a special way, and this does not imply any inferiority. They are able to assert their human existence and being in a natural way.

So writes Marie Louise Von Franz in her book, *The Feminine in Fairy Tales*.

One should acknowledging Lilith, known by some as the Queen of the Night and by others as the ancient bad girl.

Lilith was said to have been Adams first wife. She was not happy with him and left. Her reasons included him always making her lie underneath him when making love, and also demanding her complete obedience.

Eve replaced her and later Lilith was often represented in art by the serpent. (*See the sculpture at the entrance of Notre Dame cathedral depicting Adam and Eve, and Lilith as a serpent.*)

THE EROS CRESCENT SERIES

EROS CRESCENT

No one on Eros Crescent remembers exactly the moment when the words COVID-19 or Corona virus were first uttered in their houses. Needless to say, it would first have been heard on a television report and the importance of the message would have taken a few days to sink in.

The world suddenly changed. Words and phrases like lockdown and self-isolation and social distancing were suddenly in the forefront of all conversations as people enacted the requests of government and the nation to act responsibly to assist in the national objective to achieve what quickly became known as flattening the curve.

For Roger, life couldn't have been less affected. His daily routines required only that he rose from his bed, showered and shaved, ate his breakfast, went for a walk, and made sure he had sufficient pens and paper. Although it did impinge on his new paying project.

He had been asked by Desley to write another booklet similar to the one he'd written for The Club, only this was to be for The Dunking, a venue he had not yet visited or, until now, even heard of.

When Desley explained the concept and related what the setting inside the warehouse was like, Roger was very keen to get started. But the arrival of the virus put an end to that project, at least until further notice.

For Caroline and Jackie and Miranda, staying at home was what they enjoyed anyway, that is when they weren't travelling abroad or window shopping or having coffee in cafe's.

All three women had worked in executive positions in London, but moving overseas brought that era to a close, although they had been invited to join similar companies in Australia.

A top of the range coffee making machine was promptly ordered along with a supply of fair trade East Timorese Maubisse, medium blend. Browsing online shops became the new window shopping.

Instagram took on a new importance as the pandemic took hold around the world. Stories and pictures of people in isolation doing amazing and sometime ridiculous things became the rage. Jackie uploaded hundreds of images of the inside and outside of the house, earning the praise of interior designers and architects.

Helen and her husband Frederico were effected in so far as Freddy's job as a flight controller at the airport was soon to be reduced in the number of hours he worked. However, there was no threat to his income as he was on standby as an essential service. But Helen's work as a freelance Human Resources consultant to industry came to a sudden halt. She embraced online conferencing on Zoom but this was no substitute for real hands-on consulting.

Helen was also restricted in her love life, already reduced as a result of her husbands responsibilities to Helen's two lovers who had inadvertently become pregnant to him.

Sophie and Freya now spent a night a fortnight with Freddy. Unable to visit or have visits from her own lovers, Polly or Celia Ashbee, Helen would just have to manage with her next-door neighbour, Mary. And what looked like the answer to maiden's prayer, The Club had been forced to close.

Mary's only loss of employment was her volunteer job at the Salvation Army Opportunity Shop which she would miss very much. She would also miss her sensual workout with her close friend Janice. But most of all, she would miss her newly found excitement at The Club which she had only recently opened.

Her niece and housemate, Sophie, worked at a horse stud and accepted reduced hours and looked forward to doing baby things at home. Because she and Mary lived next door to Helen and Freddy, the two households would have access to each other when needed. And of course, Freddy was to be the father of Sophie's as yet unborn child.

Alice and Frey both lamented the loss of work in their jobs as school counsellors. They both loved their jobs. Both were pregnant and accepted they would be forced to spend more time at home together.

Like most of the others, they had their favourite sex toys for when they weren't knitting baby clothes or doing jigsaw puzzles. And like so many women in lockdown, they visited female friendly porn sites online. The two decided that they would always share these internet session and happily parked themselves on the sofa, transmitting the websites from their phones to the giant television set via a magic little box. This meant that the images were so big that they felt they were in the same room and this proved most enjoyable on many occasions.

Bertie and Rosa were the older folk who were most vulnerable to the virus. They were happy to be isolated although Bertie complained that he would miss his fortnightly get together for coffee and cake with Freddy and Roger.

Bertie complained that he still had much to say on the subject of breaking down the worlds dependance on the "couples model" as he called it.

"Nothing good will happen while we maintain this ridiculous habit of pairing off for life. Firstly, in over half the cases, it doesn't work and people separated or divorced.

"Secondly, it was obvious that people who stayed in these relationships were deeply frustrated by the repressive demands on them of constantly answering to another person.

"Thirdly, paternity and property ownership where the only reasons this system was maintained and with the likely end of democracy as we know it looming, house prices and pension funds and equity investments were likely to collapse.

"And I haven't even mentioned the problems of religion and religious wars."

Rosa looked at him. She loved him dearly but managed always to call him out.

"You haven't mentioned love once."

"Sex and love are two seperate things, my dear. We both know that."

Most of the close friends and relatives knew that Rosa and Bertie had broken up many years ago and taken lovers. Rosa entered relationships with her close girl friends and occasionally, a man.

Sometime later, she and Bertie got back together as a couple, but both maintained their freedom to embark on other relationships if they so chose, and this arrangement worked very well. It wasn't that they were desperate to take on other romantic adventures, but just knowing that they were free to do so, made the difference. They broke up after almost twenty years and had now been together for nearly fifty years.

"It was a necessary pause," agreed the two of them, lovingly.

The two people that were originally going to be living together but in the end chose not too, were Edith and Jessica. But living at different ends of the same street meant that they would not need to forego their times together. And they, like Maude and the others living in number nineteen, had each other for company if and whenever they wanted.

Edith and Jessica had the boys on hand and could also still get a pizza delivered, although it sometimes took a little longer.

But then they learnt that they would now be sharing the boys with the very sexually active Maude and possibly with the two new girls who moved in to number eleven just before the lock down. Jessica and Edith's plans to invite the new girls in for a pizza, were in hand.

Edith still went for her walk on Mount Eros on most mornings where she usually met her friend Chloe and the two, more than not, would spend loving time together in Chloe's secret cave.

It was thanks to the lockdown, that Jessica met Chloe. Edith had long wanted the two to meet so when Jessica was unable to attend classes, she accompanied Edith on her walks.

Jessica and Chloe were instantly friends. Both knew that the other understood Chloe's relationship with Edith. And when the rain fortuitously arrived on their first walk together, all three made haste to the hidden cave and it was only a few minutes before Jessica had Chloe underneath her on the carpet of leaves with Edith dragging first Jessica's then Chloe's shorts and panties off before sitting beside them with her bare breasts available for the occasional grope from both girls.

———————————

It was Desley who had the most to lose but she wasn't particularly put out. The Club had to close only two short months after opening and only a few weeks after Desley had formed a partnership with her friend Sally who had opened The Dunking venue. The Dunking was closed too.

Desley welcomed the opportunity to take a rest and review everything about the club and the new venture and be ready to make any necessary changes or recommendations to Sally when they eventually reopened.

She and her partner Alvie, lived on the premises. Alvie knew about Desley's dalliances with Roger who she said she also had a soft spot for.

Desley had laughed, saying that now that they had so much time on their hands, she would endeavour to entice Roger to pop in for a threesome if Alvie didn't mind sharing. To which Alvie replied that she wanted first go.

Maria and her daughter Serina were at first, forced to stay home with grandfather Aldo and the boarder, Giorgio. They mostly worked for older people as cooks and housekeepers in the stately home of Vaucluse and Woollahra.

They successfully applied for positions with the council as carers so that they could continue working.

They both had each other and the two live-in men to play with when they felt like it plus a range of toys they enjoyed.

Maud, the owner of the music school and owner of the property at nineteen Eros Crescent found isolation difficult, severely limiting her adventures although she had managed to entertain herself with young Ashton and Damian after the two became suddenly sexually aware after falling prey to pizza nights with Jessica and Edith.

And Sylvia and Stella, the two girl who she had enjoyed briefly when they stayed over on the night of her house warming party, seducing Maude with the help their bunny outfits, had booked in for music classes and accomodation the week before lockdown. Maud reasoned that maybe life wouldn't be too bad after all.

Peoples attitudes were changed in part by the arrival of the pandemic.

Australia was fortunate that it could close its borders and clamp down easily on travel.

Europe was badly affected and Britain failed in the early stages to take action which might have prevented many of the casualties they suffered.

The USA continued to be the sad case that it had slowly become.

Big enough to make loud noises but also it seemed, too big to be able to maintain good democratic government.

It was presided over by a man who couldn't cope with an enemy he couldn't see and he couldn't lash out at, or verbaly deride.

The arrival of the invisible virus was to prove his undoing.

Life on Eros Crescent went on. The residents continued to love each other in many different ways and despite the sudden disruption of the pandemic, there was a feeling of optimism in the air.

Babies were on the way and new life called out for new ideas. And new ideas about how society worked were desperately needed.

Cross your sanitised fingers everyone, and hope.

CONTACT

Publisher or review enquiries should include your full name and
details in all correspondence.

Email address:
countrynotebook@gmail.com

RICHARD LEE PUBLISHING

Erotic Fiction

New 2022:

Wet Dreams for Oldies 1: Never feel lonely again (P/back)

ISBN: 978-0-909431-23-5

Wet Dreams for Oldies 2: Never feel lonely again (P/back)

ISBN: 978-0-909431-24-2

Beatrice Part One: Secrets everywhere (eBook)

ISBN: 978-0-909431-41-9

The Eros Crescent trilogy as paperbacks or ebooks:

The Fifi Code

ISBN - 978-0-909431-02-0

Eros Crescent

ISBN - 978-0-909431-05-1

Mount Eros

ISBN - 978-0-909431-08-2

Excerpts from the Eros Crescent series as paperbacks or ebooks:

Janice: A sexual enigma

ISBN - 978-0-909431-10-5

Jessica: A young woman's journey

ISBN - 978-0-909431-13-6

Helen: Enough is not enough

ISBN - 978-0-909431-14-3

Maria: Always available

ISBN - 978-0-909431-15-0

Mary: Catching up

ISBN - 978-0-909431-11-2

The Club: Ladies love it!

ISBN - 978-0-909431-11-2

Happy Honeypots: Swinging in Harmony

ISBN - 978-0-909431-20-4

Roger: Ladies love to pay him

ISBN - 978-0-909431-21-1

Literary Fiction

Australian Short Stories

ISBN - 978-0-909431-00-6

Restless: A novel about two young men growing up in Australia between 1900 and 1936 (Publication date not set.)

Out of Print Titles

Mathematics for Young Children by Helen Western

ISBN - 978-0-909431-01-3

Currajong: For Those Whom Schools Have Failed

by Bruce Wicking

ISBN - 978-0-909431-03-7

The Puppetry Handbook by Anita Sinclair

ISBN - 978-0-909431-04-4

Wordswork by Chris Davidson & Bruce Wicking

ISBN - 978-0-909431-06-8

Sheep Production by Murray Elliott

ISBN - 978-0-909431-07-5

Ducks for Starters: A Practical Guide to

Backyard Duck Keeping by Bruce Wicking

ISBN - 978-1-875207-00-8

Sweethearts by Colin Talbot
ISBN - 978-1-875207-02-2